There's no justice, and little freedom,
in a world where might makes right…

"Company," Gar said softly, and Dirk paused in the act of
dropping his cooking gear back into his saddlebag to look up
at the armored knight who was coming up the road with a
dozen men behind him. Coll, their native guide, watched the
two foreigners with curiosity and not a little trepidation as the
knight rode up, gesturing to his men to surround the three of
them.

"I hereby impress you into His Majesty's service," the
knight said curtly.

Coll felt as though something were breaking inside him, felt
as though the scrap of hope the two men had offered were
being snatched away—then felt fear mount in its place.

Dirk said dryly, "We're not impressed."

…but where the Rogue Wizard goes,
change is sure to follow!

A WIZARD IN WAR
The Third Chronicle of the
Rogue Wizard

BOOKS BY CHRISTOPHER STASHEFF

A WIZARD IN WAR

Copyright © 1994 by Christopher Stasheff

Cover art by Darrell K. Sweet

A Tor Book
Published by Tom Doherty Associates, Inc.
175 Fifth Avenue
New York, NY 10010

Tor Books on the World Wide Web:
http://www.tor.com

Tor® is a registered trademark of Tom Doherty Associates, Inc.

ISBN: 0-812-53649-5
Library of Congress Catalog Card Number: 95-34735

First edition: November 1995
First mass market edition: July 1996

Printed in the United States of America

0 9 8 7 6 5 4 3 2

A WIZARD IN WAR

CHRISTOPHER STASHEFF

TOR®
fantasy

A TOM DOHERTY ASSOCIATES B
NEW YORK

A WIZARD IN WAR

1

Dicea didn't hear the knight approaching until it was too late—even though he was laughing and joking with his men-at-arms—so she was tardy turning her face to the wall, and the knight espied her. "*Hola!* Come here, pretty lass!" he cried, but Dicea shrank away, eyes wide. "Fetch her, Barl," he ordered one of his men, and the soldier came, grinning and reaching out for Dicea, who cried out and tried to push herself back into the wall, forearms up to shield her torso, face down in her fists.

Anger tore through her brother, Coll. He jumped between Dicea and the soldier and cracked a fist into his jaw. The man gave one surprised grunt—after all, serfs never fought back—and slumped, eyes rolling up.

The knight turned scarlet on the instant and shouted, "Kill him!" He, too, knew that serfs couldn't be allowed to fight back.

Four soldiers came at Coll. Panic seized him; he knew his only chance was to kill them first. He leaped on the foremost soldier and swung high, but the soldier was ready to block now, so Coll kicked his feet out from under him and seized his spear as he fell, twisting it from his grasp. He slashed with it at the soldiers. They leaped back in surprise and caution, knowing what that honed edge could do and how little use leather armor might be against it. Then they reddened and shouted, but Coll had just time enough to stab downward and kill the fallen soldier.

The knight shouted in rage, and his men echoed him, charging. Coll leaped to meet them, parrying the thrust of the soldier on the right, then stabbing him in the belly, just as though his spear were the butt of a quarterstaff. Serfs weren't supposed to know how to fight with staves, but Coll and a few friends had practiced in secret. Now he turned on the middle soldier, stabbing upward. The man parried, beating Coll's spear down—and Coll leaped in and cracked a fist into his chin.

The knight bellowed in anger as he saw a third man fall and spurred his horse. The charger surged forward; Coll barely managed to sidestep in time, and the rest of the soldiers came at his back.

"Behind you!" Dicea called, and Coll turned just in time to dodge their charge, then slash at one of them with his spear. The knight turned his horse and came charging back, blood in his eye, intent on running Coll down.

"Flee!" his sister cried, tears in her eyes. "Oh, Coll, flee!"

Every cell in his body screamed to stay and fight, but the knight was slashing down with his sword, and sense forced its way through the haze of Coll's rage. He leaped aside at the last second, then dodged between the peasant huts. The knight swerved to follow him, and ragged serfs stopped watching the spectacle to scramble for cover. But Coll ran a zigzag route between huts, then sprinted madly over the patch of cleared ground between the village and the woods, hearing the hooves of doom pound closer and closer behind him, imagining he could feel the charger's hot breath on his neck. He made it into the woods ten feet ahead of the horse, though and dodged and twisted among the trees, knowing he was safe now, if not for long.

Behind him, the knight cursed as he reined in, sheering away from underbrush that was too thick for his horse. "Run, fool, run!" he bellowed. "You'll make fine sport for the count and his knights, better than any deer! We'll track you down and spit you like the swine you are!"

Coll ran, turning and twisting through the wood, cursing himself for a fool indeed. He had killed two soldiers, and the hunt would be on for him in earnest; the knights for miles around would gather in high spirits to track down the insolent serf who had dared strike a knight's soldier. He had let his temper, and the anxiety that had driven him to protect his little sister, make him a dead man or, at best, an outlaw—if he managed to outsmart and outrun the knights and their hounds—and all for nothing! The knight would have Dicea after all, and would probably rape her brutally in revenge on her brother, instead of the more gentle forcing that, with men of his rank, passed for seduction—and Coll's life was forfeit, if anyone managed to catch him.

Coll resolved to make sure they never would.

Dirk Dulaine glanced at the ship's viewscreen in disgust. "*This* is how you go about choosing which planet's people to help next? Sheer random chance?"

"Not 'sheer.' " Magnus d'Armand looked up from the navigation tank across the ship's bridge, at his friend. "I eliminated all the planets that do have firm standards of civil rights, after all."

"Oh, fine! So you cut down the size of the pool to only those planets that do need help! And what did you do after that? Take the nearest one! Why didn't you just throw dice, or put the names of the planets on a dart board?"

"How would you recommend I choose, then?"

"Oh, I don't know . . . Maybe you could prioritize, for example?"

"An interesting thought!" Magnus stroked his chin, gazing off into space. "By what criteria should we prioritize? The degree of oppressiveness of the government?"

"Sounds good. How can you determine it?"

"A nice question. Historically, some governments have been more oppressive than others. An unchecked aristocracy, for example, tends to allow more individual exploitation than a monarchy. A king tends to keep the noblemen in check to some degree, at least, and a person wronged by his lord can apply to the King's Justice if he feels unjustly treated. The Roman dictatorships certainly had the potential for great abuse, but in actuality, the dictator was held in check by his fellow patricians, especially in the Senate. And the Greek tryants, of course . . ."

"All right! All right! You've made your point!" Dirk threw up his hands. "We could debate all day and still be wrong! Any form of government could be balanced by local factors."

"Oh, I'm not saying it wouldn't take a lot of thought," Magnus protested. "It would be worth it, though, if it brought us first to the ones who needed us most."

"Yeah, but while we're taking a year or two thrashing it out, thousands of people could be dying on the planet we finally decided to help. I see what you're doing—better to save some now than none eventually, even if they're not the ones who need it most."

"Need it most? Yes, maybe we could do it that way!" Magnus clapped his hands, smiling with delight. "An index of human misery! That shouldn't be terribly hard to compile. Herkimer, show us examples of human misery."

An hour later, Dirk, pale and trembling, laid down his notepad and stylus. "I surrender. If my planet had had to wait for you to work your way down this list of sheer human degradation, you wouldn't have made it to us for another five generations."

"But your idea does have some merit to it!" Magnus looked a bit feverish himself. "There has to be some way to say which of these poor human scraps are more miserable than the others!"

"I can't see much difference in the treatment this last dozen are getting from their lords," Dirk contradicted. "They're all living like animals in huts made of leftovers from the harvest, freezing in winter, soaking or parboiling in summer, and half starving all year round. They're dying of scurvy and beriberi and half a dozen other vitamin deficiencies; their brains are only half grown due to infant malnutrition. Their lords drive them to work with whips and scourges, rape the few pretty girls they produce, and punish the slightest sign of rebellion with torturous deaths that I can't call barbaric only because I don't want to insult the barbarians! Just take one of them at random, Magnus, please! We've got to get some of these poor bastards out of their misery, or I'll never sleep nights again!"

"Yes, I agree." Sweat stood out on Magnus's brow. "Still, your index of misery is a brilliant idea. We do seem to have found the dozen worst cases of all."

"Definitely worst! At least my people had enough to eat and decent clothes to wear, and the lords only took the prettiest girls—and didn't rape them, just seduced them. Okay, we were humiliated at every turn and treated as though we were semiintelligent conveniences, but at least we didn't live in misery like this! I hate to say it, but we didn't know how good we had it!"

"No," Magnus contradicted, "you just didn't know how bad some other people had it, or how much worse off you could be. Well, let's take the planet with the continual warfare for starters. There, I don't see any sign of the fighting ever letting up, and it's grinding the serfs to bits. What do you say we try to work a small revolution on the planet Maltroit?"

"*Small* revolution? A big one, please! The biggest you can manage!"

"No, that would only result in a change of masters," Magnus objected, "not to mention another bloodbath while they switched places. A small revolution can produce a big improvement in living conditions right away, and an even bigger improvement with each generation. Herkimer, set course for Maltroit."

Dirk sat down again, frowning. "How can a small revolution make a big difference?"

Magnus began to tell him. Dirk kept asking questions, so the explanation became more and more involved—but Magnus did manage to wrap it up as they went into orbit around Maltroit, five days later.

The guards formed a hollow square around the king's herald and conducted him into the great hall, where Earl Insol lolled in a huge chair of carven oak. The message was quite clear: if the sentry said words that offended, the guards would become jailers, or worse. The king's man put on an urbane smile to hide his indignation. The impudent lord wouldn't dare defy His Majesty!

Would he?

Still, he squared his shoulders as the two guards stepped aside and pointedly did not bow as he said, "Good afternoon, my lord."

Insol frowned; the herald should have known better than to speak first. No doubt the fool thought of himself as embodying the majesty of the king who had sent him, therefore being at least temporarily equal to the earl. "What says the king?" he demanded, brusquely and with no preamble.

The herald fought the urge to scowl at the man's rudeness. Didn't His Lordship know he was mistreating not just the herald, but also he who had sent him? "His Majesty sends me to tell you of one Bagatelle, my lord, a dealer in cloths and fabrics."

The earl's eye gleamed; he recognized the name. "A common caitiff? What of him?"

"This Bagatelle appealed to our noble king of this land of Aggrand for justice, claiming his goods had been stolen, and himself beaten, by yourself, my lord Earl. His Majesty summons you to his court, that he may hear from your own lips whether or not you have flouted the King's Peace, and dealt so roughly with one of his subjects."

The earl sat very still for a minute. Then he said, "Summons? Did you say that this child of a king dares summon an earl twenty years his senior?"

The herald reddened; he was scarcely into his twenties himself. "His is the king!"

"And an impudent upstart he is," the earl retorted. Then his voice became velvety smooth. "Might he not invite me? Ask me to wait up on him?"

"He has no need! He is the king, and all of his subjects must obey!" But the herald was beginning to have a very nasty feeling about all this.

"It is time this arrogant stripling learned the limits of his power!" the earl snapped. "Ho, guards! Take this impudent chatterbox to the dungeons and strip that gilded cloth from his back!"

As the guards laid hold of him, the herald went pale. "How dare you defy your sovereign lord!"

"Very easily," the earl said with a wolfish grin. Then, to the guards, "Do not begin to flog him until I am there."

He came quite quickly, and watched, gloating, as they batted the herald from one to another with their fists, as though he were the ball in a game. He watched while the torturer flogged the youth, watched as his men dressed the poor moaning lad in grubby peasant's leggins and led him out into the courtyard to tie him, stripped to the waist, on the back of a donkey. Then the earl caught the herald's face in a viselike grip, squeezing on the points of the jaw. "Tell your royal master that he overreaches himself. Tell him that he may not summon his lords, but may invite them with all due courtesy. Tell him to mind his manners henceforth, or his nobles will fall upon him as they fell upon his grandfather, to whip him back within the boundaries of his own estates!"

Then he let go of the herald and swung a riding whip at the donkey's flanks. The beast brayed in pain and alarm and leaped away, running, with the poor herald clinging to its mane for dear life. Cavalrymen rode after him, laughing and whipping the donkey if it strayed off the road that led back to the royal demesne.

"The king cannot let this insult pass, my lord," said the oldest of his knights as he watched the donkey bear its bruised and bleeding load away.

"He cannot indeed," the earl agreed. "He shall come against us, and we shall whip him home shrewdly." He shrugged. "He had to be taught sooner or later, Sir Durmain. Best to have it out of the way, so soon after his coronation." He watched the donkey out of sight, then turned to the knight. "Send reports of this event to every other duke and earl in the land, so that each may gird himself for war."

Coll fled from the hounds, but his knees had already turned to jelly, and his whole body seemed to be liquefying with fatigue. All night he had been making his way through the woods, trying to hide his trail well enough so that the knights wouldn't find him, but as the sun neared noon over the forest, their hounds had somehow picked up his scent. They weren't near yet, but it wouldn't be long. Their belling was growing steadily louder.

In a last attempt to lose them, Coll jumped down into a stream. The water was icy so early in the spring, and he knew he couldn't walk it for long without his feet turning numb. But he kept going, shivering and cursing, hoping to find something that might save him . . .

There it was, a boulder jutting up from the water with a low-hanging evergreen branch above it! Coll clambered up the boulder, slipping and falling back twice because his feet were already losing feeling and because he was already exhausted. Finally he stood on the boulder, trembling, and raised his spear in shaking hands—but not shaking so badly that he couldn't catch the crosspiece of the spear in the fork of the branch. Now, if only the crosspiece would hold, and the branch, and his hands . . .

He couldn't. He was too exhausted; it was all he could do to hold the spear in the fork of the branch. To haul himself up so far was beyond him.

Then the hounds' voices suddenly became much louder, and he could hear the beaters shouting, "On, Beau! On, Merveil!" and a knight crying, "Take half of them across! Trace both sides of the bank till you find where he came out!"

Too close by far! Panic shot strength through his arms; Coll climbed up the shaft hand over hand as quickly as any squirrel, caught the branch, and pulled himself up to lie trembling on it, panting. He hauled up the spear one-handed, then clung to the smaller branches, his feet lying on others, feeling his perch sway beneath him, waiting for his breath to slow, for the fear and panic to ebb. The fear didn't, for the pack was coming closer and closer . . .

And going by on the bank, not five yards from where he lay hidden among the needles! Coll clung tight and prayed that there would be no breeze to carry his scent to the coursing hounds. The saints must have heard him, for the dogs went right on by, belling, their beaters calling encouragement to them.

Then they were gone.

Still Coll clung to the branches, gasping, feeling sobs in

his chest, fighting not to let them out, for he knew that if they began, they wouldn't stop, and he didn't dare make that much noise, or the pack might come back.

They did. He clung tight, trying to breathe silently through his mouth, hoping against hope that they would go past again . . .

They did. He breathed a prayer of thanks to a kind and forgiving God, and went limp.

In the depths of the night, a star detached itself from the firmament and came spinning down toward earth. As it came lower and lower, a watcher on the ground would have seen it swelling into a great golden disk, not a proper star at all.

Of course, there *were* no watchers, if you discounted the small herd of wild horses sleeping in the spring night. The absence of witnesses was one of the reasons the ship was landing in the middle of a moor. The horses were another.

A slice of the ship's underside separated and dropped down, forming a ramp for Magnus and Dirk.

"All right," Dirk said, hoping his nerves weren't showing. "How do we go about this?"

"You mean you've never caught a horse before?"

"Only tame ones." Dirk held up the rope he was carrying, eyeing it with distrust. "What do you do with a wild one?"

"Convince it that you're its friend, and that it wants to carry you where you want to go. That's the easy part."

"The *easy* part?" Dirk said with great trepidation. "What's the *hard* part?"

"Getting the chance to get acquainted." Magnus shook out his own rope, forming a lariat. "Let me show you how it's done." He marched off across the plain. Against his better judgment, Dirk followed.

When they came in sight of the horses, Magnus slowed

down amazingly. Then, quietly and very slowly, he began to move toward the sleeping herd.

The breeze shifted, and the lone, waking horse sentry looked up, nostrils flaring, staring straight at Magnus, every muscle tense.

Magnus stared back.

Dirk could almost see the tension flow out of the horse, saw it calm amazingly, and knew that Magnus, the telepath, the expert in every psi power known to man (and in most of those known to woman, too), was reaching out with his mind to soothe and reassure the horse's mind. More than soothe—slowly, the horse lowered its head. Then, quite relaxed, it folded its legs, lay down, and went to sleep.

"Now," Magnus breathed, "we pick the ones we want, and set a lasso around each one's neck."

"You mean *you* do," Dirk corrected.

The sentries saw the herald coming a mile away—or rather, saw the donkey with someone on its back. But their suspicions woke as the two horsemen who accompanied the beast turned away and rode in the direction from which they had come. The sentries told the captain of the guard, and the captain sent out two riders to see what the donkey carried. When they saw, one stayed trying to revive the herald before bringing him in, while the other rode back with the news.

The young king himself came down to see the herald as he rode through the gate. Black eyebrows drew down in anger as he looked at the man's bruises, at the dried blood in the welts on his back. The herald managed to raise his head enough to croak, "Majesty . . . Earl Insol says . . . you exceed the limits of your power . . ."

"There *are* no limits to a king's power!" His Majesty struck the swollen face with the back of his hand; the herald's head rocked, and he would have fallen off the donkey if the ropes had been untied. The king turned away in disgust. "Put him to bed and see that he is tended."

The herald croaked pathetically, and the captain said, "Majesty, do you not wish to know the rest of his message?"

"I know it from his condition," the king snapped. "Earl Insol will not come to me—so I shall go to him, with my army! Send couriers to each of the knights of my demesne, that they must come to me straightaway with a hundred men-at-arms each!"

"As Your Majesty says." The captain's face was expressionless, hiding his foreboding. "Shall I also summon your lords?"

"The lords? Fool, they are more likely to march against me than for me! It was the lords who leashed my grandfather, and it is the lords who must be taught my power! It is for this that my father made more and more knights all the days of his reign. Now it is for me to use them! Earl Insol shall be the first! Summon my knights and their men, and we shall teach him the limits of *his* power!"

Coll crouched among the rocks, watching the lone monk amble toward the outlaw's hill on his donkey. Coll stared at him with hungry eyes—and a hungry stomach. Oh, he had eaten better than ever he had as a serf, far better—but he would gladly have traded all his fresh meat for gruel with good companionship to sauce it.

Still, that was not to be, so he was glad to see a prospect of something better—two prospects! It seemed unbelievable, but in the month he had been hiding in the wastelands, he had come to realize that life sometimes did play tricks like this. A week since anyone worth robbing had come along that trail, and the food from the last one had run out two days before, two days in which he had eaten nothing but the little rodents who burrowed around his hill, and the occasional hawk who came to prey upon them. Now, in a sudden embarrassment of riches, there came three at once, two from the east and one from the west! The road curved around his hill, so he was sure neither saw the other, and decided he would have time to rob the monk before the knights came in sight—though he would have to use the back trail down his hill, for the knights were sure to come after him as soon as the friar went crying to them. At least they weren't armored—but he could tell by their clothing that they were knights indeed, or, at the very least, reeves. Not that he feared them—but there was always bad luck. One alone he would have braced without a thought— he had become adept at unhorsing knights in this last month—but two was far too risky.

So! Rob the monk and be done with it, quickly. Down the hill Coll went, as nimbly as any of his ground squirrels. He knew the route well now, knew on which boulders he dared catch himself and which he dared not. At the bottom, he crouched behind a boulder set on top of another boulder—his hill was more a rock pile than an earth pile— and waited.

The monk came ambling along on his donkey, singing a ballad that had little of the sacred about it. Coll sprang down in front of him, brandishing his spear. The donkey shied, and the monk screamed, fumbling for his purse. "Don't hurt me, don't hurt me, wild man! You may have my purse, all the copper that's in it, even a coin or two of silver!"

"What use is money to me?" Coll snapped. "Where should I go to spend it? No, fat man, it's your saddlebag I'm after! Bread and cheese and wine, and anything else you have stored in there that I can eat!"

"Eat? Oh, I've something far better for you to eat here under my robe!" The monk fumbled under his cloth— then tore it open as he drew the sword hidden beneath, revealing a chain-mail coat as the cowl fell back to show an iron helmet. "Taste steel, robber!" he shouted. "Ho, my men! Out upon him!"

Suddenly they were there, leaping out from behind boulders: a dozen armed soldiers in leather breastplates and steel caps. In a flash, Coll realized what had happened, realized it even as he leaped back among the boulders of his hill and scrambled to get out of sight. The knight had sent his soldiers across the plain the night before, while Coll slept, then come himself at first light, before Coll might have discovered the deception.

But they were stiff from crouching all night, those soldiers, and Coll was warm and nimble. They came charging up among the rocks, shouting and slipping. Coll braced himself against one of the unstable boulders, threw all his weight against it, and the knight cried out in dismay as the huge rock rolled slowly toward him, gaining speed. He had to forget Coll to turn his donkey aside—but the soldiers didn't. With a whoop, they converged on Coll.

With a sinking heart, Coll knew his end had come—but with a vast relief, too, that his lonely hiding was over, and a savage joy that he could take one last revenge on the knights and their lackeys. He sent up one quick prayer of contrition, begging to be forgiven for the men he was about to kill in a vain attempt to save his own life, then swung his sling twice around his head and loosed. The pebble struck the nearest soldier in the forehead, knocking him down even as the blood began to flow; then Coll dropped the weapon and blocked a slash from the next soldier, blocked it and returned it, slicing the man's arm open. The soldier howled and fell back, but that left more room for the other eight, and they fell on Coll in a shouting mass. He blocked and slashed with his spear until it was wrenched from his hand, saw the sword coming up to thrust through his bowels even as four hands seized his arms and shoulders from behind . . .

The yell echoed all about him, the staves knocked the soldiers away, the tough shaggy ponies struck out with hoof and tooth—and suddenly, Coll stood alone, half the soldiers fallen and the other four backing away in fear of the two knights who rose over him on their horses. Incredibly, the smaller was saying, "Hang in there—and pick up your spear again. They won't try anything against the three of us."

The bigger man—not big, huge!—was answering the outraged challenge from the knight in the monk's robe. "Who are you who dare to seize this outlaw from us!"

"Outlaws ourselves, though well-dressed ones." The tall man dismounted. "I am an outlaw who was knighted once, though, so there's no shame in fighting me. However, a horse against a donkey is unfair and unworthy, so we'll fight on foot, shall we?"

The disguised knight took in the size of him, seven feet tall and broad as a wall, and took a few steps back. "You're much bigger than I am!"

"Yes, but you're wearing armor, and I'm not." The huge knight leveled his sword. *"En garde!"*

2

The knight shouted with anger and spurred his donkey. His men yelled with him and charged the giant's companion.

Coll shouted in anger of his own and leaped in beside the shorter stranger. He whirled his spear like a quarterstaff, striking aside one sword after another. The donkey took one look at the man-wall wielding a sword and sat down where he was. The knight gave a yelp of surprise and half-fell, half climbed off the beast. The giant laughed and stepped in, slashing. It was a halfhearted cut, but enough to make the armored knight scramble to guard and swing his sword to parry. Then the two of them set to in earnest.

Coll parried two more blades, not quite far enough—one of them grazed his arm, but he ignored it, not caring which stroke killed him, for he had known he was dead from the moment the false monk drew his sword. He saw a half-second's opening and struck with the butt of his spear. It jabbed into the belly of the man to his left; he fell back with a grunt of pain—but another soldier stepped over him and struck. Coll barely had time to parry the thrust from his right before he had to turn the jab from his left, then snap his shaft up to block a blow from the front. He kept the movement going, though, bringing it down hard to his right, stabbing into the shoulder of his attacker just as the man was starting a strike of his own. The soldier dropped his spear with a yell of pain, and Coll fell to one knee, ducking under the stroke from his right, feeling the blade graze his cheek, waking pain, but he came up to stab from below at the man in front. His spearhead found blood; then his shoulder struck the man's midriff, carrying the soldier into the spear of the one behind him.

Now Coll was free, leaping and turning at a fourth soldier. Another slammed into him from his side; agony streaked the back of his shoulders, but he drove his spear butt into the man's belly, then yanked it back and cut with his spearhead as though it were a sword, slashing the arm of the soldier who had been on his right. The man staggered back, howling and clutching his wound, then tripped over one of his companions and fell.

And, suddenly, it was over, except for the two knights. The shorter stranger stood in the midst of three fallen soldiers, blood staining his sleeve and running down the side of his face, but the grin he gave Coll was sure and strong. Coll found himself grinning back. Then they turned together to watch the duel, both ready to leap in and help.

There was no need; it was clear the bigger man would already have won if his opponent hadn't been wearing armor. As it was, blood was seeping through the chain mail between breastplate and hip guard, and the giant's doublet was streaked with crimson. But the big man fought only with a rapier and dagger, where the knight hewed at him with a two-handed broadsword.

The giant leaped back from a particularly vicious slash, grunting, "Save it for an oak!" The knight stumbled after his sword, off balance, and the stranger stepped in with an extra push! The knight cried out and fell, but he rolled onto his back quickly, slashing as he rolled. The giant swung hard, knocking the sword on down to the earth, where he set one big foot on the blade. The knight cursed, trying to tug it free—then froze, seeing the sword tip poised over the eye-slit in his visor.

"Surrender," the big stranger said softly, "or I strike."

The knight cursed him again and shouted, "Strike, coward!"

The stranger's eyes narrowed, but he held the blade poised and said, without looking, "Dirk, shell this lobster for me, will you?"

"Come on," Dirk said to Coll, and stepped forward to begin unbuckling the knight's armor. The man cursed him furiously, but didn't dare move for fear of the sword aimed at his eyes. Coll grinned and stepped in to help.

They threw the plate aside, revealing a heavily muscled man in a sweat-stained gambeson.

"Now the helmet," the big man instructed, and pulled the sword tip back just long enough for Dirk to yank the helmet off the man. The knight was yellow-haired and hard-faced, with cold grey eyes, a scar on his lip, and murder in his eyes.

"Back," the big man instructed.

"Anything you say, Gar." Dirk stepped back.

So did Gar. "Get up," he said to the knight, "and take your sword." He cast his own aside.

The knight stared in disbelief, then gave a gloating laugh as he scrambled to his feet, caught up his sword, and struck.

Gar danced back; the blade hissed by an inch from his chest. Before the knight could recover, Gar leaped in, caught his wrist on the backswing, and jammed the man's elbow against his own. The knight cried out in surprise and pain; Gar twitched his arm, and the sword fell from nerveless fingers. Then the big man leaped back, letting the knight stumble free. He rubbed his arm, glaring up at Gar, and spat, "Son of a chancred whore!"

"Pleased to meet you." Gar bowed. "Myself, I am a son of a lord."

The knight's face went purple at having his own insult turned back on him; he shouted with inarticulate rage, starting toward Gar—then pivoting and leaping at Dirk.

Coll stood frozen, taken by surprise, then shouted—but even as he did, Dirk swung his arms up, breaking the knight's hold, then cracked a fist into his jaw. The knight stood poised for a moment, then fell and lay still.

"Sorry about that," Gar said.

Dirk shrugged. "Accidents will happen. Next time, forget the stunts and just take out the competition, okay?"

"Comment noted," Gar confirmed, then turned to Coll. "I hope you're worth all this trouble, stranger."

"Not to mention a few flesh wounds." Dirk turned to Coll, too. "Of course, you took your share. Who are you, anyway?"

Coll stared at them, suddenly realizing that two total strangers had saved him. "Only Coll," he said, "only a runaway serf and murderer." He raised his spear to guard. "For your help, I thank you—but why?"

Gar ignored the spear. "We don't like seeing one man attacked by a pack."

"No, definitely not," Dirk agreed. "Of course, there's also the little matter of our needing a guide. We're from out of town, see, and we figure we can get around quicker if we have someone who knows the territory."

"Why . . . I can guide you through the lands for ten miles about," Coll said slowly. "I've come to know them well, in this month of running and hiding. Beyond that, though, I know no more than you do—and if the lords find you harboring an outlaw, they'll have your heads!"

Dirk shrugged. "They'll have to take them first. Besides, how do we know you're a criminal? You just bumped into us on the road—what did we know?"

Gar pulled tunic and hose from his saddlebag. "Whoever thought that a man dressed so well could be on the run?"

Coll stared. "For me?"

"Well, you'll have to take a bath first." Dirk drew a bottle from his saddlebag and came up to Coll, pouring some of the fluid onto a square of cloth. "Of course, we'd better see about those cuts. Hold still—this will sting."

Coll eyed the cloth with misgiving, but stood his ground. Dirk wiped his shoulder, and Coll gasped with pain, then set his teeth, determined not to cry out. Instead, he managed to say, "You really mean to take me as your servant?"

" 'Hire' is the term," Gar said helpfully. "You may not know the territory very far away, but you do know which lord is which, and who hates whom—and I suspect you could make a rather shrewd guess as to which will attack the other."

Dirk stepped back, turning some sort of black cap onto the bottle in place of a cork, and Coll relaxed; the stinging was already passing. "Who will attack?" He shrugged. "Any of the lords. But they will attack the new king, not one another. They have been patching up their feuds ever since he was crowned, getting ready to teach him his place."

Gar raised his eyebrows. "I thought your noblemen were always fighting one another."

"They are, and it's a blessed rest," Coll told him. "Of course, Graf Knabe is still fighting Count Gascon, and Duke Vladimir is defending his border from the raids of the Marquis de la Port—but their families have been fighting for as long as anyone can remember."

"So they certainly wouldn't stop for a mere little thing like a coronation, eh?" Gar asked.

"Of course not," Dirk answered. "Why waste a perfectly good feud?" He turned back to Coll. "So it's going to be one of the lords attacking the new king, eh?"

Coll shrugged. "Unless he attacks one of them first."

"In which case, they'll all pile in on top of him?"

"They might," Coll said slowly, "but they also might sit back and wait till he is weakened. If His Majesty wins, some others will look for excuses to attack him, while the neighbors of the losing lord divide up his estates."

"Sure. Why not wait till they're both weakened?" Dirk said.

"No reason that I can think of." Coll didn't seem to recognize sarcasm—or didn't see any place for it. "Some of the village elders favor the one, some the other. One or two do think the lords will all attack the king without waiting for cause, though."

"Quite a country," Dirk said to Gar, "when every peasant with a few years' experience could teach a course in political intrigue."

Gar shrugged. "We learn what we need, to stay alive." Then to Coll, "However, since Dirk and I haven't learned yet, we'd like to take you along as a teacher."

Coll gave a harsh laugh. "Teacher? When was a serf taught to read or write?"

"Only after the revolution." Dirk's face hardened.

Coll frowned. "What is a revolution?"

"The peasants getting fed up with the lords," Dirk explained. "No, I think you have all the qualifications we need. What's your name, by the way?"

"Coll," the outlaw said, bemused. "But I tell you, I know nothing!"

"And we tell you that you know everything we need to learn," Gar corrected. "Besides, we can be sure whose side you're on."

"Yes, you can." Coll's face was stone, but turned to confusion again as he blurted, "How can you trust me, though? I'm an outlaw! A killer!"

"What kind of choice did you have?" Gar asked.

"I could have let a knight take my sister," Coll said grimly, and felt the bitterness rise again. "He probably did, anyway."

Gar and Dirk exchanged a glance. Dirk gave a nod and turned back to Coll. "Yeah, we can trust you. Now about that bath . . ."

Dirk helped Coll bathe—helped by giving him a cake of real, actual soap, some sort of oily potion to clean his hair—then some brown liquid to rinse it with. Gar gave him a length of soft, fluffy cloth to dry his body. As Coll pulled on the leggins—no, hose!—he protested, "What if someone from my village should see me? Or one of my lord's men?"

"They won't recognize you," Dirk assured him, "or did you have those scars on your face before you left home?"

"Well . . . no." Coll hadn't thought of that.

"Besides, they all know that Coll has yellow hair." Gar drew a polished circle of metal from his saddlebag. "Look!"

Coll looked at the circle, and saw a face looking back. He stared in shock—it looked very little like the face he had seen staring back from the still pool only a month before! It was hardened, scarred—and topped with brown hair! He looked up at Gar wide-eyed. "What magic is this?"

"Hair dye," Gar explained, "though it does look a little odd with that yellow beard. We're going to teach you a new skill, Coll."

The serf stared up at him. "A skill?"

"It's called 'shaving.'" Dirk unfolded a strange, square-ended blade from its hollow wooden handle. "You do it with a razor, like this. Hold still, now—this won't hurt much."

Which was more or less true, at least compared to being wounded with a spear—but it hurt enough that Coll was dismayed to hear he was going to have to do it every day. When he looked in the mirror again, though, he didn't recognize himself at all. Why, he was bare-faced as any knight! Or at least a squire . . . "You were right! Even my neighbors would never know me now!"

"I'm sure they wouldn't," Dirk agreed. "Still, it never hurts to make sure. Which way is your home village, Coll?"

Coll pointed to the west. "That way, on Earl Insol's estates."

"Then we'll go east." Dirk mounted his horse. "What lies that way?"

"The king's own demesne," Coll answered.

Dirk and Gar exchanged another glance. "Well," the big man said, as he mounted his tall roan, "no matter who attacks whom, we'll be there to see it. Do they hire extra soldiers, Coll?"

"Free lances? Yes, and there are many of them riding the roads." Coll frowned. "If they can't find work, they turn bandit—and far more cruel than I've ever been, from what the minstrels sing!"

Dirk nodded. "That's the kind of work we're looking for. You can still change your mind, Coll. You don't *have* to come along."

Coll looked back at his hill and thought of the knight and his men who would be coming to about now and discovering the dead bodies among them. "Thank you for the choice, fine gentleman—but when I think it all through, I find I would just as soon come with you."

The tunic and hose were made of good stout broadcloth, better than any Coll had ever worn.

By midafternoon, they had come out of the wastelands and were riding through farmland that had been fruitful sometime in the past. Now, though, the rolling fields were littered with broken spear shafts and wagons, lying on their sides or in pieces, rotted spokes drooping from wheels that no longer had their iron rims. Among them lay the bones of horses and oxen, picked clean—and even, here and there, the bones of men, some with rags of livery still clinging to them, flapping in the breeze. Occasionally they saw a broken spearhead or halberd blade; all other iron was gone, scavenged.

The wreckage clustered along lines where armies had met and fought, lines that divided the fields in place of the hedges that had been trampled underfoot. Peasants were plowing those fields again, as the needs of life triumphed once more over the profligacy of death.

"This was a hard battle." Gar gazed out over the fields, his face somber. "Who fought whom?"

Yes, they were outlanders. "Count Ekhain and Earl Insol," Coll told them. "The wasteland is Count Ekhain's; the little river that borders it also borders these rich lands of Earl Insol's—or lands that *were* rich, once."

"So Count Ekhain tried to take them, and Earl Insol fought him off," Gar interpreted. "Did Ekhain have any excuse?"

"Excuse?" Coll stared. "Why would he need an excuse?"

"Why indeed?" Gar murmured.

"Some sort of justification, maybe?" Dirk prodded.

Coll shrugged. "What justice could there be in war?"

"That plowman." Gar nodded toward the nearest field, where a grey-headed man with a white beard wrestled with a share. A boy ran along beside the beast's head with a switch, shouting at the animal now and again to keep it in a straight line. "Isn't he a little old to be cutting a furrow?"

"Yes, but what choice has he?" Coll replied. "All the young men and the fathers are away at war. Who is left to guide the plow but the grandfathers?"

Gar shuddered. "Let's hope the war will be over soon!"

"What matter?" Coll shrugged again. "There will be another one in a few months."

Gar turned to stare at him. *"Always?"*

"For as long as I can remember, at least," Coll told him, "and my father before me." Really, he was beginning to think these men weren't just strangers—they must be simpletons, too, not to see something so obvious. Wars end? How could wars ever end?

Of course, they might not have been simpletons, but simply from very far away indeed. For a moment, excitement stirred in Coll's breast. Could there actually be places where wars did end? Where a whole county or duchy might find ten or twenty years of peace? But he shrugged off the notion almost as soon as it came. Fairies and elves were real—everyone knew that, even though they had never seen them—but a land without war? Impossible!

Dirk nodded at the plowman, his white hair tousled by the wind. "How old is that grandfather? Sixty? Or only fifty?"

"Fifty!" Coll stared, amazed. "Few serfs indeed live to *that* age! No, sir, that man is surely only thirty-five, perhaps forty at the most!"

Dirk stared, and Coll could see that he was unnerved.

"I would age early too, in such a land," Gar said gently.

Dirk swallowed thickly and nodded.

Coll was all the more flabbergasted. Surely they were crazed! Surely there could not truly be a land where plowmen lived to be sixty! A lord might live that long, but surely not a serf—and to still look youthful at thirty-five? Impossible!

A similar thought seemed to have occurred to Gar, because he turned and asked, "I had thought *you* were in your thirties, Coll. How old are you?"

"Thirties?" Coll stared, wondering if he should take offense. "I am twenty, sir!"

"Indeed." Gar sat gazing at him for a minute, then nodded and turned his face back to the road. "I think we chose the right place, Dirk."

"I should say we did!" Dirk averred, and came after him.

Coll followed Dirk, wondering.

Then he saw the woman sitting by the roadside with a

miserable, scrawny child clutched to each side of her, and anxiety stabbed him. How long before Earl Insol warred against the king? How long before the soldiers reached Coll's mother and sister? For surely the knight would already have sent Dicea home grieving . . . His blood boiled at the thought, but Dirk's voice distracted him, even though he was speaking in a low voice, to Gar. "How old is the woman?"

"I would have said fifty," Gar replied, "but judging by what Coll's been telling us, she can't be more than thirty."

Coll glanced at the woman and nodded.

"Are those boys or girls?" Gar's voice was still pitched low. "Or one of each?"

"Can't say, just by looking," Dirk replied, "but I'd guess they were five years old, both."

"So skinny . . ." Gar shuddered.

Coll looked more closely, and felt a stab of pity. These were children who had never known a time without war, without soldiers marching through their village—and never known a day without hunger, or with enough to eat. He wondered if their father still lived, and if so, with which army he marched.

The woman raised bleary eyes at the sound of the horses' hooves, then pushed herself to her feet with a sudden burst of energy, cupped hands outstretched. "Alms, good sirs! A penny for the children, a heel of bread, a crust!"

"More than that!" Dirk said with indignation, even a little anger. He pulled a loaf from his saddlebag.

Gar touched him on the shoulder. "Not too much. They're starving . . ."

Coll frowned. Surely, if they were starving, that was all the more reason to give them as much as they would take! But it was the knights' food, after all, and if they didn't want to share too much, who could blame them?

Dirk gave a curt nod, broke off the heel, and handed it

to the woman. She took it eagerly and started to break it, but Dirk said, "No. One for each of you."

The woman froze, staring at him, amazed.

Dirk broke off another piece, and another, taking up half the loaf, and handed them down. "Here, eat." As they began to gobble the bread, he looked a question at Gar, who nodded, and Dirk turned around to dismount. "Some broth would help." He took a pot and a handful of rods from his saddlebag, and a small box with them. Stepping off the road, he unfolded the rods and set a ring with four short legs on the ground. He kindled a fire beneath it, set the pot on top of it, poured in water from his water bag, took a cube of something dark from the box, and dropped it in. The woman watched him with curious, avid eyes, and as the water began to boil, she sniffed the aroma of beef broth with delight. "It has to boil," Dirk told her, "then cool— but it will be good to drink."

The children pressed in, half hiding behind their mother, staring at the pot with famished eyes.

"Are your children boys or girls?" Dirk asked with a gentle smile—but the woman stiffened with alarm, clutching both little ones to her as she rattled, "Boys, sir, both boys!"

Coll wondered why Dirk seemed so startled. Surely he must know that any girl had to be protected from the lords' soldiers, no matter how young.

"They're fine young lads of ten and twelve," the mother assured Dirk. Coll understood why the knight seemed so startled, so troubled, for he had heard him guess at their ages.

Mother and children were sitting by the roadside, eating a little more bread and drinking the broth from wooden mugs, when harness jingled, and horse hooves sounded on the road.

"Company," Gar said softly, and Dirk paused in the act of dropping his cooking gear back into his saddlebag, to look up at the armored knight with his dozen men behind him, coming up the road toward them. Dirk mounted his horse as Gar said in a hard, low voice, "Take them into the woods, Coll."

"Go along with you now!" Coll shooed the mother and children off the road and into the trees. They turned and ran, still holding their mugs. Once behind the screen of leaves, Coll called, "Finish your broth, leave the mugs, then go as quickly and quietly as you may."

The woman nodded, wide-eyed; the children drank off the rest of their ration, and the mother brought their cups to Coll. He gave her a curt nod, never taking his eyes from the roadway, never turning to watch them lose themselves in the woods. He was far too concerned with watching the knight ride up to Coll's new masters, gesturing to his men to surround them, saying curtly to Gar and Dirk, "I hereby impress you into His Majesty's service!"

Coll felt as though something were breaking inside him, felt as though the scrap of hope the two men had offered were being snatched away—then felt fear mount in its place as Dirk said, loudly and dryly, "We are *not* impressed."

3

Say you so, bumpkin? Then have at you!" the knight cried, and couched his lance.

"My meat," Gar told Dirk. "You keep the riffraff off my back."

Dirk only nodded and spurred his horse wide to the side.

The knight gave a shout and spurred his mount. The huge animal lumbered into motion, then shifted up quickly from trot through canter and into full-fledged gallop. The footmen gave an enthusiastic shout and loped after their master.

Dirk cut across them, swinging a sword that certainly shouldn't have been sharp enough to cut through their pike shafts—but it did, clipping them off like a scythe through wheat.

Gar sat his horse calmly, waiting as the knight bore down on him, lance point centered directly on Gar's chest, shouting, "Yield, you fool! Yield, or *try* to run!"

"I would almost think you didn't like taking people's lives," Gar called back—then suddenly made his horse leap aside to the left. He caught the shaft of the lance as it went by and pulled. By rights, the knight's momentum should have yanked Gar off of his mount, but horse and rider both set their heels, and the knight whipped about in his saddle as the leverage of the long lance twisted him to his right. He clung to it like a bulldog until pain wrenched his midriff, then dropped the lance with a howl and turned back to his horse just in time to slew it around in a great curve. Gar waited until he had turned and was on his way back before he held up the lance in both hands and, with a sudden heave, broke off the first two yards.

The knight shouted in anger and spurred his charger. It thundered down on Gar as its master lugged out a broadsword and swung it two-handed at Gar's head—which made it possible for the the giant to duck under the blow, then come up to throw his arms around the knight. With a crash and a clatter, they both shot out of their saddles and hit the ground.

The footmen slewed to a halt and stared, amazed, at their headless weapons. They looked up at Dirk, an almost superstitious fear coming into their eyes.

It certainly rose into Coll's heart. What kind of steel was his employer's sword made of, anyway?

Then one of the soldiers plucked up a bit more courage than the rest and came at Dirk with a shout, swinging his headless shaft like a baseball bat. Dirk grinned, made his horse sidestep at the last second, and chopped another foot off the staff as the soldier blundered by.

But he had put some heart back into the rest of the men-at-arms, who must have realized Dirk couldn't dance away from them all, for they charged the lone horseman with a shout.

But Dirk had changed weapons—he was spinning a loop of rope over his head. Seeing him without a blade, the soldiers decided he was easy meat, and charged with a gloating cry.

Dirk rode a dozen feet in front of them, crossing their

path; his lasso spun through the air and fell around the shoulders of the soldier in the center. He yanked it tight, and the man slammed into the soldier next to him—who slammed into the man next to *him*, then back against the one behind as Dirk rode in a circle around the whole dozen of them. They shouted in surprise and dismay as the rope yanked them all together like a sheaf of wheat, staffs knocking one another on the head, jumbled together so tightly they could scarcely breathe. The horse pivoted and threw its weight back, digging its hooves in to keep the rope taut.

Gar helped the knight to his feet, then picked up his sword and handed it to him. "Fool!" the knight snarled, and swung the blade high, two-handed. Gar retreated, drawing his own weapon.

But Coll saw a lone soldier rise up from the grass and run to catch up the cutoff end of the knight's lance. It was six feet long, and he leveled it as a spear, charging at Dirk's back in silence.

"Behind you!" Coll shouted, then ran to catch the fellow even as Dirk turned to look. He saw the lance coming just in time and leaned to the side; it skimmed past his ribs, tearing cloth. Then Dirk caught the shaft and pulled. The soldiers stumbled, off balance, and Coll swung his staff, knocking a very solid blow into the man's skull.

"Well struck!" Dirk said with a grin. The knot of soldiers cried out, protesting; even through the attack, Dirk and his pony had kept the tension on the rope. One soldier fumbled his belt knife out and tried to reach up to saw at the cordage, but it held his forearm pinned, and he could only curse as the knife slipped from his fingers.

Coll glanced at Gar, and saw him dancing in and out, avoiding the knight's sword chops, while the man of metal lumbered after him, panting like his own horse. Coll could hear the harsh rasping of breath even through the visor— Gar was breathing hard, too, but certainly not with any pain; he was even grinning! Striped here and there with blood where he had moved almost quickly enough, but grinning nonetheless . . .

The knight blundered forward with one more slash that had all the deftness and skill of a Clydesdale hauling a broken beer wagon. Gar sidestepped, then pivoted in close, his dagger flashing. The knight shouted and stepped back, stumbled, wavered, but kept his footing—and his breastplate swung open, the straps on the left side cut! Gar lunged across the man's body, then riposted before that huge cleaver of a sword could catch him—and the right shoulder of the breastplate fell down, leaving the knight's torso exposed, but with the armor shell still hanging at his hip to foul his movements. He shouted in rage, lunging at Gar and swinging down hard. The giant gave a shout of glee, sidestepped and parried the blade down so that it struck into the ground, then thrust with his own sword. It came away with blood on the tip, and crimson stained the knight's gambeson. He stared down at it in disbelief.

"Only a flesh wound," Gar said, "unless there is less meat on your chest than I think."

The knight threw himself at Gar with a roar. The big man sidestepped; the knight blundered past, stumbled, and fell. Gar reached down, caught a shoulder, and turned him over. He didn't even have to raise his sword; the knight held up both hands, crying, "I yield me! I yield me!"

"Why, then, there shall be peace between us," Gar said slowly, though he did not sheathe his sword. He did lean down, though, to catch one of the knight's arms and haul him to his feet.

"If that's how you fight without armor," the knight asked, "what could you do if you wore a proper harness!"

"A good deal less," Gar replied frankly, "for it would slow me down and restrict my movements greatly. I must admit, though, that I do favor a chain-mail shirt in battle."

Coll watched with bitterness. It was all a sort of game to them, these knights safe in their iron shells—and if that game went wrong, they could end it by surrender. Not so for a poor serf hounded into lawlessness—or even a serf pressed into an army for battle. For him, the fight went on and on to the death.

"Throw down your weapons," the knight called to his men, "for it is knights that we fight, not merchants or villeins!"

Reluctantly, the men-at-arms dropped their staves—all that was left of their pikes. "Go find your steel," Dirk told them, and let go of the rope. They thrashed and pushed their way out of the knot of men, then spread out to find and pick up their spearheads and halberd blades.

The knight turned back to Gar. "I am Hildebrandt de Bourse. Whom have I had the honor of fighting?"

"Gar Pike," the giant said, with a small bow, "and I am honored indeed to have crossed swords with so doughty a warrior as yourself, Sir Hildebrandt."

Sir Hildebrandt returned the bow, apparently not realizing the humor in the name Gar gave—but Coll did, and had difficulty throttling a laugh. Gar Pike, indeed! And a most amazing fish he was, too!

"So you know us for what we are," Gar said, amused. "Is it only because I know how to duel?"

"That," Sir Hildebrandt agreed, "but I know you also by your chivalry; you could have slain me by nothing more than a thrust that cut deeper by inches, but you chose not to—then honored my surrender, and even set me on my feet."

Yes, chivalrous and merciful, Coll agreed silently, *to another knight!*

"I rejoice in meeting a man of enough gentility to recognize me for what I am." Gar inclined his head. "However, though I am a knight, I am one whose lord was slain in battle, and am therefore without house or lands. I live by my sword and my wits now, pledging myself to whatever lord needs me."

"And your friend, too?" Sir Hildebrandt looked up at Dirk, who nodded. "Well, if you are true free lances, I cannot think to impress you into His Majesty's army—but I will offer you his shilling, and the chance to win his favor."

"How pleasant an invitation!" Gar grinned broadly. He glanced at Dirk, who nodded, then said to Sir Hildebrandt, "We will be honored to accept! Tell me, whom are we to fight?"

"Earl Insol," the knight answered, "for he has most grievously insulted our king."

Coll heard the words with a sinking heart. Visions of his village rose in his mind, visions of it burned and smoking, of the cottage trampled into the mire—mud reddened by the blood of his neighbors—and of Dicea struggling in the arms of a soldier, who laughed through a gloating, gap-toothed smile as he displayed his prize to his mates. Yes, Coll felt a bit of resentment at having his destiny decided by these two strange knights without asking him—but he was far more pleased to be in the army that would attack Earl Insol. Perhaps, if he could be one of the first soldiers to reach the village, he might protect his mother and sister—and warn his neighbors.

Sir Hildebrandt led them to a river, then south along its banks until they came to a broad road. At the river's edge, it slanted down to a ford. There were guards at that ford, wearing blue tunics with a silver lion rampant on each.

"What does that livery mean?" Dirk asked Coll. "Whose is it?"

"The king's." Coll eyed the soldiers with some awe: he had never seen the monarch's troops before. "The blue is the color of the royal household."

"So you were hiding in wastelands that were just barely out of Earl Insol's demesne?" Dirk gazed out across the water. Forty feet away, on the farther bank, stood guards wearing red. "Whose color is that?"

Coll swallowed. "Earl Insol's—my former master."

"I take it this river is the border of the king's estates?" Gar asked. The outlaw nodded.

Insol's men stood with their backs to the river and to the royal guards—but one turned and called across, "What's the hour?"

A royal guard glanced at a sundial, then called back, "Not yet noon. We must go hungry a while longer, eh?"

"It's enough to make a man bait a hook," Insol's man grumbled.

"The soldiers don't seem to have anything against one another, at any rate," Dirk commented.

They followed Sir Hildebrandt toward the east, on a well-packed road through fields of ripening grain. Coll couldn't help but think that those stalks would soon lie trampled in the mud, with soldiers' bodies among them. So much labor wasted! So many lives! So much hunger!

They camped for two nights, and Gar and Dirk struck up conversations with the soldiers, who seemed surprised to find themselves forgiving the men they had sought to kidnap—but Sir Hildebrandt talked to the stranger knights by the hour as they marched, so they could tell themselves they were only following his example. Coll just sat and watched, saying as little as possible, and realized quickly that Dirk and Gar really didn't say much about themselves—only enough to lead to the next question, and to bring the soldiers to talking again. Coll decided that was why everyone enjoyed talking to them so much: they listened well.

Of course, if Sir Hildebrandt and his men had known why the two strangers paid such close attention to everything they said, they might not have taken so much pleasure in talking—and from the comments Dirk and Gar made, Coll saw how quickly they were learning about the land.

They were learning so much that Coll decided they had originally known even less than he had thought. It was amazing they spoke with such slight accents.

Halfway through the third morning, Coll looked up and saw a castle's turrets rising above the ridge ahead of them. He caught his breath, awed at the thought of actually seeing the royal stronghold. Unable to believe it, he turned to the soldier next to him and asked, "Is that the King's House?"

"King's House?" The soldier grinned. "Aye, lad, and if that's a house, I'm the giant Tranecol!"

Coll took his meaning and smiled. "Bigger than my mother's cottage, eh?"

"Summat bigger, yes," the soldier allowed.

As they came closer to the ridge, though, the turrets seemed to sink below it, so that, as they came to its top, the royal castle seemed to burst upon Coll's eye, its towers reaching for the sky, its curtain wall stretching a mile wide, its moat a veritable lake.

"Impressive," Gar murmured.

"You would find it very much so, if you sought to take it," Sir Hildebrandt assured him. "The moat is fresh and fed by springs within it, so there is never a lack of water, and its granaries are always full. That drawbridge rises in several sections, and those battlements can rain scalding water on any who come close enough to raise ladders."

"It's almost as though it stands on an island, not as though a ditch has been dug about it," Coll breathed.

"It *is* an island," the soldier told him, "and you could grow enough grain to feed an army in its courtyards, if the soldiers didn't need them for drill."

Another soldier nodded behind him. "That wall's seven hundred yards long, lad, and I should know, for I've paced it time and again on sentry-go, counting my steps as I went."

Coll believed it more and more as they came closer until, as they came to the gatehouse that stood on the land-ward end of the bridge, the castle seemed to fill the whole

landscape. The sentries challenged them, but saluted when
they saw Sir Hildebrandt's colors and stepped aside. They
rode through the sudden darkness of the short stone tunnel, with its arrow slits to either side and the slits in its roof
for pouring down hot oil, then rode out across the cause-
way, where the castle filled the whole world. Sentries challenged them again from atop the inner gatehouse, then recognized Sir Hildebrandt and cried a welcome. They rode
through the chill of another entrance tunnel, longer this
time; then sunlight struck them as they came into outer
bailey.

Coll stared; he had never realized so huge a space could
be enclosed by a man-made wall. Far away against the eastern side, knights rode at quintains. All about the walls, hammers rang and forges belched smoke. A troop of soldiers
practiced halberd play with quarterstaves, and serfs loaded
wagons with barrels and boxes. Coll could feel the thrill, the
apprehension and excitement; this was the home of an
army preparing for war.

Lackeys ran to help Sir Hildebrandt dismount; he tossed
his reins to one and turned to beckon to Dirk and Gar.
"Come! You must meet your new liege lord."

They dismounted, but Coll sat more firmly, willing his
saddle to hold him as though he were glued to it. Sir Hildebrandt saw, though, and ordered, "Come, man! Will you let
your masters go unescorted?"

Dirk gave Coll a glance of commiseration that had the
firmness of command to it. The serf sighed, and followed
his knight-friends up the stairway that climbed the side of
the keep, into its great, gaping door.

A liveried footman bowed as they entered. "Welcome,
Sir Hildebrandt. We have announced your coming to the
king, and he awaits you in his chambers."

Coll was surprised that Dirk and Gar were *not* surprised;
their land couldn't have been so very different from his,
after all. For himself, he knew, as everyone did, that it was a

sentry's job to report all who come as soon as they were in sight, and a herald's job to know every knight by his coat of arms.

"May I know the names of your companions?" the herald asked.

"You may," Sir Hildebrandt replied. "They are knights from a distant country, come over the sea to fight for His Majesty—Sir Gar Pike and Sir Dirk Dulaine. Their squire is one Coll."

"Be welcome, gentlemen." The herald gave Dirk and Gar a deferential nod, then turned back to Sir Hildebrandt. "If you would be so good as to follow, I shall announce you."

Sir Hildebrandt gave a curt nod. "Lead on."

They followed, Coll half dazed, his heart singing within him. A squire! Could he truly be a squire? Surely not, for neither Dirk nor Gar had told him he was any such thing! But if the herald wished to make the mistake, why, who was Coll to correct him? A mere serf, that was all—certainly not a squire!

They walked through halls as high as any cottage's roof and halted at an elaborately carved door of dark wood, flanked by guards. The herald said, "Sir Hildebrandt, with two strange knights and a squire."

The left-hand guard nodded. "You are expected." The other guard swung the door wide. The herald stepped in and announced, "Sir Hildebrant de Bourse, with two new-comers, Sir Gar Pike and Sir Dirk Dulaine, with their squire Coll."

"Show them in," snapped a resonant baritone.

The heralds stepped aside and bowed Sir Hildebrant in. Gar and Dirk followed with Coll behind them. "Majesty!" Sir Hildebrandt bowed. "May I present Sir Gar Pike and Sir Dirk Dulaine, newly come to our land of Aggrand from a country far across the sea."

Dirk and Gar stepped forward to bow. Coll bowed, too,

but stayed back as far as he could, wishing he could slip behind a tapestry—but staring at the king nonetheless.

He wasn't very impressive, really—no taller than Coll, and only a few years older. He stood behind a table spread with parchments—or paced, rather, pausing every now and then to look down at a map pinned there, then look up again, eyes flashing with anger. His long hair was glossy black, as was his jawline beard. He wore a short surcoat of purple velvet trimmed with ermine over a brocaded doublet of scarlet embroidered with gold thread, and scarlet hose. His face was set in a look of simmering anger as he glared at the map, his eyes black, his nose Roman over fleshy lips. His crown was scarcely more than a coronet, padded with more purple velvet trimmed with ermine, but it held a jewel in every point over a band of precious stones.

"From a far country?" the king asked. "What is its name?"

"Melange," Dirk replied. "There was a war, and our noblemen lost. We thought it wise to travel for our health and seek our fortunes by our swords."

The king smiled. "You, at least, might do better to live by your wit."

"Doesn't every courtier?" Dirk countered.

The king actually laughed, a short, harsh bark. "True, Sir Dirk, but few of them have much to work with there. What of you, Sir Gar?"

"I fear I must leave lightness of heart and quickness of lip to my companion," the giant said in a soft voice. "I have little to recommend me but my sword."

Somehow, Coll knew that was anything but true, and Dirk reinforced that opinion. "His sword *and* his gift for organizing a battle, my lord. Some men know where the bodies are buried, but Gar always seems to know where to find the live ones."

The king laughed again, a little more freely this time. "Let us put you to the test, then, Sir Gar. Come, look at this map and tell me where Earl Insol shall attack, and how I may counter him!''

Gar stepped around the table beside him, pursing his lips as he gazed down at the map.

4

Gar placed a finger on the map. "Is this the river ford we passed on our journey here?"

"You came from Sir Hildebrandt's manor in the north? Yes, it is." The king seemed surprised that Gar had found the intersection of road and river so easily.

"You'll have it heavily defended," Gar predicted, "and if I can see that, so can the earl. He won't even try a crossing, though he'll mass enough soldiers there to make you think he will. No, he'll send his troops across the river at least a quarter mile away."

The king stared at the map in surprise, then frowned and demanded, "How?"

"In boats," Gar said.

"With horses? It would take far too long!"

Gar nodded. "Even so. He will send only a dozen knights by boat; the rest will be foot soldiers, but they'll be his most experienced, his best. They'll make enough trouble for ten times their number, and draw your troops away from the ford. *Then* his men will cross—but they won't be the main body of his troops, just enough to keep your army busy, and while they're distracting you, the rest of his soldiers will cross the river here and here"—he stabbed the map with the forefinger of each hand, wide apart—"these two fords. How distant are they from the main road to your castle? Four miles?"

"A bit more." The king stared intently at Gar.

"Close enough to arrive before the diversion is over, then. And Insol will cross at both fords, so that he can bring his troops marching around like the pincers of a crab's claw, with your troops between them as they shut."

"You have guessed even as I have." The king watched Gar narrowly. "I will have troops hidden in the forest nearby, of course, to fall upon them as they come out of the water. What else will I do?"

"Why, carry the fight to Insol, of course!" Gar said, surprised. "Your army will be ready before his, will it not?"

"It will indeed, especially since the knights near those estates will gather there rather than here." The king turned to Sir Hildebrandt. "You will command the force that guards the center ford, though, Sir Hildebrandt. Keep half your force here; send the others back to Northford."

"As Your Majesty wishes." Sir Hildebrandt bowed his head, keeping a straight face.

The king turned back to Gar. "So my army shall attack from north and south at the same time, fording the river and charging out upon Insol's hidden forces. What shall they do then?"

"Catch them sleeping, since your men will cross under cover of night. I would guess that you would send your best soldiers across first, dressed in black and moving as silently as possible, to take out Insol's sentries, so that you can catch his camps by surprise. When they've slain or captured all his soldiers and knights, your forces will wait for dawn, then ride posthaste to attack his castle. With luck, you may catch him before his drawbridge goes up."

"Exactly as I had planned!" The king clapped his hands in delight. "This is a most insightful recruit you have brought me, Sir Hildebrandt! Can he fight as well as he plans?"

"Oh, he most surely can," the knight said ruefully.

"But can you lay schemes beyond a battle?" the king asked.

"Strategy, Your Majesty means? Yes, I have some knack for it, if I am given full knowledge—but I know little about your country or your barons, and less about your goals. Do you go only to chastise one earl?"

"That's as must be," the king said grimly. "If Insol's defeat is enough to make the rest obey and send the full tax that they owe, and soldiers for my personal army, well and good—but if not, I shall have to chastise each of them, one by one."

"To what purpose?" Gar pressed. "For gold and strength of arms? Or to curb their harsh treatment of their serfs, and make them instruments of your own justice, not merely their own whims?"

"Gold, of course, and the strength to compel them to do as I command! Why should I care how they mete out their justice, or how they herd their serfs? Such cattle are good only for tilling the land and gathering wood, nothing more!"

Coll clamped iron control over his whole body to keep it from shaking with rage.

"But those 'cattle' are human," Gar said softly, "and make foot soldiers for your army, and mothers to raise more soldiers."

"They must be tended with care, of course, as any cattle must! Do you think I know nothing of husbandry?"

"Of course not, Your Majesty," Gar soothed, "but to guess at your strategy, I must know how many serfs you wish to keep alive when your war is ended."

"As many as possible, of course! What good is a field with no one to plow it?"

"Then you wish to make the barons stop fighting one another, and wasting serfs in the process?" Gar pressed.

"Wasting! What manner of talk is that?" The king made a chopping gesture. "What care I how many cattle they slay in their wrangling? Let them fight each other every day of the year, weakening one another so that they may fall easy prey to my armies, when I wish to compel them to obey!"

"Then the constant warfare that assails this land *is* your strategy," Gar inferred.

The king stared in surprise, then slowly grinned. "Most insightful indeed." He turned to Sir Hildebrandt. "The man is a marvel, Sir Hildebrandt, and more than fit to command! See to it that he leads the charge across the northern ford, and that Sir Dirk is beside him!"

"Of course, leading the charge will almost guarantee that you're killed in the battle," Dirk pointed out, "especially if your soldiers aren't any better fighters than that." He pointed at two squadrons of footmen who were practicing halberd play with wooden weapons—and missing one another as often as they struck.

"Of course," Gar agreed. "The last thing a king wants is a really capable knight leading a body of well-disciplined, hard-fighting soldiers. This king may be a brute, but he's no fool."

Coll stared at him, scandalized, feeling cold runnels of fear all through himself. Then he glanced frantically to left and right, to see if anyone was close enough to hear—but Gar and Dirk had chosen the right location for a private talk; they were ostensibly surveying the castle and the soldiers, so they were out in the middle of the courtyard, where no one could hear them—except Coll, of course, but he shared their opinion of the king. He had hoped to find a wise and compassionate young monarch, filled with ideals and burning to stop the slaughter of serfs in the lords' petty wars. Instead, he had found a man who was perfectly willing to encourage those battles, and wanted only more gold and more power. Coll's rage smoldered in him like a banked fire.

"He's intelligent," Dirk pointed out.

"Oh, yes, intelligent," Gar agreed. "If he weren't, he wouldn't be half so dangerous. Intelligent and shrewd."

Dirk nodded. "The kind of man who thinks you can trick your way around morality."

"No, he doesn't even *think* about right or wrong. After all, he knows he's the king."

"So anybody who opposes him is wrong?" Dirk asked.

"Only in his own eyes."

"I see," Dirk said softly. "He *is* his own morality."

"Which is another way of saying that he's a selfish, egocentric brute," Gar said dryly.

Coll wasn't sure what all the words meant, but he *was* sure he agreed with them. Like Dirk and Gar, he had found his king to be very disenchanting.

Dirk noticed. "You don't look any too happy about him either, Coll."

The serf shrugged. "You, at least, can leave this land, if you don't like its king, sir."

"Dirk," the knight corrected.

"Dirk." Coll tried to smile. "You can leave. I have to live with this king."

"Yes." Dirk's eyes narrowed; his voice dropped. "But *he* doesn't."

Coll stared, trying to understand what the knight meant. When he realized it, it struck him like lightning, and he staggered. The idea that people could rid themselves of a bad king was shocking, worse than shocking.

"Steady." It was Gar's hand that held him up. "After all, you're an outlaw."

Coll stared at him, uncomprehending. Then he understood what Gar meant, and he felt a rush of strength swelling within him as a wolfish grin tugged at his lips. He was dead already, if the law caught him—how much more dead could he be for fighting against the king?

"He's young, though," Gar reminded Coll. "We might still make something of this king of yours."

Coll stared, even more flabbergasted. How could you re-make a king?

"Is he a pretty good example of the men who rule you," Dirk asked, "or are the lords any different?"

The question took Coll aback. "I only know of Earl Insol."

"But you must have heard something of the others."

Coll shrugged. "From the rumors we hear in our village, they're all the same—not the songs the minstrels sing in the common, but the words they speak in low voices when the door is barred and the night keeps folk home in bed. All of the lords want wealth—who doesn't—and all of them want power, or they wouldn't be lords."

"That makes sense, as far as it goes," Dirk admitted. "The question is, do they want anything *but* wealth and power?"

"Of course," Gar said, with a hard smile. "They want the things that wealth can buy and power can compel—rich food, fine wines, young women for their beds . . ."

Anger flared in Coll. "Yes, they're like that, all of them! Oh, my grandfather told me that Earl Insol was noble enough when he was young, that many of them are—but a year or two of power changes all that. Before his father died, the earl was angered by our sufferings; he brought us food when he could, and made his soldiers treat us more gently, so my grandfather said. They thought it was because he was in love with one of the serf girls, but dared not touch her, for she was very pretty, and his father might want her for his own—and sure enough, the old earl took her, and the young lord was too much ashamed to take her afterward.

He still came to help the serfs with food and medicine when he could, but something had died within him.''

"What happened when they buried his father and he became earl in his own right?" Dirk asked.

Coll shrugged. "He stopped the scourgings and demanded fewer days of labor on his own lands—for a year or two. Then Count Sipar, his neighbor to the north, marched against him, and he had to haul men from the plow and jam them into boiled-leather armor."

"He won, though?"

"He didn't lose," Coll sighed. "He still holds Insol. He held the border, yes, but he didn't march into Sipar's lands. At home, he began to become hard as his father, and little by little the scourgings came back, and the days of labor went up again, until we were no better off than before."

"And *his* son?" Dirk asked.

"Which one?" Coll said bitterly. "He has a dozen, among our serfs—but never by the woman he loved in his youth, they say."

"He hasn't married, then?"

"Only two years ago, and long we had to labor to provide his feast! His wife's with child at last, so mayhap there *will* be a son soon."

"And his lady?" Gar asked. "Has she come among you to cure your ills, or asked her lord to lighten your burdens?"

"Lighten them! She's calling for another day's labor every fortnight, to build the new tower she fancies!" Coll shook his head slowly. "Yes, some of them are noble enough when they're young, sir knights—but power changes that. In all of them. I've never heard of a one who used it to help his serfs—not one."

Dirk gave Gar a lugubrious look. "It *is* worse than home!"

* * *

They had only two weeks to weld the king's forces into a single army. His Majesty employed Gar and Dirk as couriers, riding from one knight to another to take them the king's orders and bring back information. It took Gar only one day to figure out that the king expected him to coordinate the bands, inducing them to work together somehow. He left it to Dirk to soothe ruffled feathers and convey orders without being too insulting, while Gar devoted himself to calming and flattering the king while he provided him with advice on tactics under the guise of guesswork. Coll rode first with the one, then the other, amazed at the number of details they gave him to work out, and even more amazed to discover that he could do every job they gave him.

In spite of it all, he still managed to squeeze in a couple of hours of drill with the king's spearmen every day, and quickly discovered that he and his friends had worked out more ways to use the weapon than the professionals had been taught. He undertook the task of teaching them, without letting them know. "Foul? I'm sorry. I never thought it would be a foul blow to strike at the belly with a spear butt. We do that at home in Melange, all the time. How did I do it? Well, you stab with the blade, but as you draw the spear back, you swing the butt down, like this . . ."

Gar watched them drill and was pleasantly surprised. "Well done, Coll, well done indeed! It seems we chose better than we knew when we recruited him, Dirk!"

"Oh, well, I always had an eye for talent," Dirk drawled, with a gleam in his eye—and a manner so droll that Coll shouted with laughter. It felt good to laugh again, even once.

Then they were marching, and the time for laughing was done.

* * *

The king himself led the crossing of the ford on the main road. He led a charge with a dozen knights behind him in the grey light before dawn, out of the water and into the earl's camp. Insol's army was just waking, just beginning to stumble out of their tents to throw kindling on their banked fires and blow them to life. The king's army swept in among them, clubbing unarmed men aside with contempt. Knights came running from their pavilions with swords already drawn and only mail coats for protection, shouting and haranguing their men into some semblance of order and bullying their soldiers into catching up spears. But the king's troops parried their thrusts, then stabbed in return, and men died. Death screams filled the air, and some of them came from king's men, for the earl's soldiers came awake quickly with the surge of fear. But they were too few and too late; the king's knights swung from horseback and struck the swords out of the hands of the earl's knights, though here and there an earl's man thrust upward and slipped his blade between gorget and helm; there and here, a king's man struck, not caring where, and a knight lost an arm or fell with blood pulsing from his throat. But most of the earl's troops fled, and in less than an hour, the king's soldiers were rounding up prisoners.

"An excellent action, Majesty," Gar told the king. Coll, overhearing, thought that Gar should have known if anyone did—after all, the plan had really been his.

"Thank you, Sir Gar." The king fairly beamed, pleased; he had won his first battle. "I trust Sir Hildebrandt and Sir Hrothgar have fared as well as we."

"I'm sure they have, Majesty," Gar told him. Coll wondered how the big man could be so certain of it.

Nonetheless, the couriers came riding at the gallop to tell of victory, and that before they were more than a mile farther down the road, with the prisoners already on their way to the king's dungeon. The king was beside himself with glee. "A triumph! A wonderful triumph!"

"It is indeed," Gar agreed, "but when we chase Earl Insol on his home estates, I trust Your Majesty will be more careful of your person—and more thrifty with your men."

The glee vanished on the instant. "What do you mean?"

"We must find some high place," Gar counseled, "so that you may look down on the battle, and direct it. I know it will be hard for you to give up leading the charge yourself, but our chances of winning the battle are greater if our tactician can see the enemy's movements and counter them during the battle, rather than setting everything in motion and hoping he was right."

The king had started nodding before Gar was more than halfway done. "Yes. A most excellent idea, Sir Gar. You will stay by me, though, to guard me."

Coll fancied he caught an undertone of relief in the king's words—and he thought Gar's sigh was entirely false as he said, "I must do as Your Majesty wishes, of course." After all, Coll reflected, Gar hadn't said who the tactician was.

So it was that, when they met Earl Insol's army, the king was no longer at their fore. Instead, he sat atop a hill with his bodyguards, Gar at his right hand, and directed the battle. There was a fair amount of grumbling about it, covering outright fear: How sure of victory could the king be, if he was so anxious to be far from his own army? But Dirk rode from knight to knight, explaining in very loud tones how the king's being away from the battle improved their chances of winning, and each knight nodded as though he had reasons of his own for agreeing. The troopers, seeing how thoroughly their masters were of one mind, began to relax and gain heart.

The earl, marching his main army to join the advance guard he had sent to the ford, had met and rallied the routed soldiers, gathering them in. Spies in the enemy camp sent word to the king that the nobleman was shocked and angry to find the king had already attacked and had captured half his advance guard to boot. "Not necessarily a good thing," Dirk explained to Coll. "He knows he has a real fight on his hands now, and is out for revenge besides."

Soldiers who overheard him exclaimed with delight, but Coll felt a cold pool of apprehension growing in his belly. It would be a harder fight than the last, much harder.

It was. The earl borrowed the king's technique from the reports of the battle at the ford, and charged at first light. The king's men were ready and waiting for him, though, and gave ground at the center of the line, fighting desperately as they retreated—desperately, because the earl's knights fought with the energy of anger, driving their footmen all the harder, and because the earl himself laid about him with furious strokes of his sword, calling for the coward king to come out and fight. The troopers could only try to parry his blade and retreat before him and his huge armored horse, because only another nobleman was allowed to battle him. Any knight who had been so rash as to try it and win would have been hanged for his pains.

Coll watched it all happen, for he crouched in the bracken high on the hillside with the rest of the reserves, hearing the king rage at Gar, "He insults me, he impugns my honor! Don't tell me again about the soldiers he has hidden in the ranks near him who are to disembowel my horse and bear me down . . ."

"The earl will be quite willing to hang them after the battle, as honor dictates," Gar reminded him.

"Then let them die—but let it be in battle, from the spears of *my* soldier guards! Live or die, I *must* fight him, or none will ever follow me again!"

"Look!" Gar pointed. "The earl has driven our center in so far that our flanks are behind his now! Yes, Majesty, by all means, charge in to fight him, for we have him surrounded now!"

The king drew his sword and charged down with a shout. His men echoed it and pelted down the hill after him, Coll in their midst.

They struck the earl's army like a hammer through thatch. The knights commanding the flanks saw them coming, and timed their own counterattack so that suddenly the earl found his army hard-pressed from every side. Even the men who had been giving ground before him were standing firm now, even beginning to press in! And worst of all, here came that idiot boy in his shining armor, plowing through the press of peasants and roaring Insol's name! There was no help for it, chivalry dictated that the earl turn aside from trying to push back the serfs in front of him, to meet the stripling in combat. "Dag! Vorgan!" he called to the two nearest knights. "Press this rabble back! I must see to the scullery boy!" He turned, couching his lance, and saw a lane open up as if by magic, foot soldiers pressing back to reveal the young king at the far end, lance leveled. Insol shouted and charged.

So did the king.

They met with a fearful crash. Insol felt his lance torn from his arm and reeled in his saddle, his stomach suddenly roiling as the sky and army swerved and soared about him. Motion stopped; dimly, he was aware of serfs turning his horse about, and pulled himself upright in the saddle in time to see the young king turning to face him, throwing aside a broken lance and drawing a sword.

Anger came to Insol's aid. He drew his own sword and spurred his horse, shouting an angry insult. The king's horse lumbered into motion, and king and nobleman met to trade blows.

But while the king was keeping Earl Insol busy, Gar was shouting orders to the other knights, who drove their men in, cutting Insol's army into wedges—wedges that fought back with the desperation of cornered men who expect no mercy, and the battle disintegrated into half a dozen skirmishes. The knots of men broke apart, and Insol's men ran for ground that gave them a better chance. The king's men raised a gloating shout, and charged after them—but the earl's serfs knew the terrain and stopped to fight again atop a ridge, so that the king's soldiers had to charge uphill at them. They met spears, and many died.

Coll didn't wait to get caught up in trying to catch a fleeing foe. As soon as he could, he broke off from the battle and ran for home. He was dreadfully aware that the fighting was far too close to his village, and that fleeing soldiers might very well run for the cover of its cottages.

5

Coll broke loose from the knot of men, slipped into the trees, then trotted as fast as he could over the old, familiar game trails. He wished he could go faster, but dared not—a storm might have washed away soil to expose a root, or a fallen branch might block the trail; he would get there faster, and in better shape to fight, if he went slowly enough to see what lay ahead. At least the enemy would have to stay on the road as they fought one another, though he knew that any who managed to break away, as he had done, would probably know the woods as well as he. When they were boys, they had paid little regard to the border between the two estates, running back and forth between villages to visit, and the king's serfs knew the trails as well as the earl's.

He burst into the village to find it silent, cold, and empty; no children played between the silent huts; no women sat in the village square, gossiping while they carded and spun. Every door was closed tight, every window shuttered.

None of it deceived Coll for a moment. Just the year before, he had himself barricaded the cottage and hidden when the alarm had sounded; he knew how the peasant folks strove to survive when the soldiers came. The only question was whether they had hidden in the woods this time, or indoors. He ran to his mother's hut and pounded on the door. "Mother! Open! It's Coll!"

There was no answer. He told himself not to be surprised, that she couldn't believe his words. He kept knocking, crying, "It's Coll!"

Was that a step he heard behind the door? Perhaps, but more clearly and more loudly came the roar of fighting men and the clash of steel. Coll spun about, to see the earl's men tumbling into the village, racing for the false security of a hut and a door. Hard on their heels came the king's men, kicking doors open and smashing them down, running into the huts to drag out screaming women and children—and the occasional soldier who had managed to hide.

Coll knew what would happen to those women when the king's men were sure they had defeated all the earl's men— for the king had been crafty; these were men from the north he had sent to attack here, not local boys who knew the villagers. He took his stand by the door, and as a king's man came running up, shouted, "None here—the hut is empty! Search the next!"

The man nodded and sped away—but three earl's men spun toward him. "Empty?"

"Let us in!"

"Aside, king's man, or die!"

A halberd swung down at Coll's chest.

He blocked it with his spear, spun the butt into the man's stomach, kicked the next attacker in the knee—but was slow leaning aside from the third's spear thrust, and the blade gazed his shoulder. It jarred into the wood of the doorframe, though, and slowed the man long enough for him to realize whom he was fighting. "Coll!!?"

"The same, Wand! And if my mother's hut is empty, I'll eat its thatch! Go find some other place to hide!"

"But what are you doing in . . ."

"Go! Don't you hear me? Run for your life and hide!"

Wand swallowed thickly and said, "Tell me later!" Then he turned and ran, dodging away among the huts.

Behind him, the door opened a crack, and his mother's voice said, in disbelief and wonder, "Coll?"

"Yes, Mother." Coll risked a quick glance. "Are you safe?"

"For now, yes." Tears choked her voice.

"And Dicea?"

"Safe, Coll," his sister's voice said, amazed and wondering. There was a shadow of movement behind his mother.

"Stay inside and bar the door, then. I'll keep the king's men from coming in!"

"But you're a king's man yourself! How?"

Three men in earl's livery rounded a nearby hut and ran pell-mell toward Coll. They didn't see him yet. "I'll tell you later! Bar the door now—these will need more than talk!"

"Bless you, son!" his mother said, and the door slammed shut.

The earl's men saw a lone king's man standing in front of a hut. Their eyes lit with relief and revenge-lust; they shouted and charged Coll.

They were all strangers—from the south, most likely. Coll swung aside to his left, beating down one spear as another thudded into the door. "For the king!" he cried, and struck his spear shaft against the nearest soldier's throat, then cracked the butt into the forehead of the second man as he struggled to yank his spear loose. But the third had taken the time to leap around both, and Coll saw the spearhead ramming straight toward his belly. He twisted aside at the last instant, and the spear only scored his ribs—but a hard fist came around and exploded in his face. The wall struck his back, and all he saw was a field of exploding lights against midnight blue. He staggered, flailing his spear out of sheer reflex—but when the stars faded, he saw the earl's man hovering in front of him, waiting for a chance for a clear blow. Behind him, a knight rounded a hut with half a dozen earl's men behind him. "The murderer!" he bellowed. "Kill him!"

Coll's heart sank, for he recognized the voice, and the coat of arms on the shield. It was the knight who had sought to take Dicea, the knight whose men he had killed!

But he struck with his spear, stabbing and swinging, and downed three men before the others struck him a stunning blow. He fought to hold on to consciousness in spite of the roaring in his ears, fastening his attention on the hard hands that yanked his arms up behind his back, bowing him over, for the pain helped him stay conscious while the stomach-lurching swirl of colors faded. It did, and the roaring dimmed; he found himself staring at the ground, the shouts of anger and fear and the din of swordplay filling his ears. He threw himself back and upright, feeling something, someone behind him crushed against the hut wall, heard him cry out—but none of it meant anything because, wonder of wonders, there was Sir Gar in his mail shirt, hammering at the earl's knight with his broadsword. Coll knew it was Sir Gar because his shield held his device—blank, matte metal, except for a black armored horse's head in the center. Behind him, Sir Dirk wheeled his horse and wheeled again, slashing at the men-at-arms with his rapier.

Behind, but quickly before. The soldiers cowered back, spears uplifted to defend themselves, and Sir Dirk swung his horse about to come charging down straight at Coll! The soldier behind him shouted and dodged aside, letting go of Coll, and the serf tried to step aside, but he stumbled, and the horse was coming straight at him . . .

At the last second, Sir Dirk pulled back on the reins, and the horse reared, whinnying protest. It swung about sideways, dropped down, and Dirk reached an arm to Coll. "Climb aboard, quick!"

Coll could only stare in amazement for a moment. Then he leaped, catching Dirk's arm and clambering up onto the stallion's rump. Turning, he was amazed to see Sir Gar's sword flicker in past the knight's guard, stabbing into the crevice between arm and breastplate. The knight cried out in pain and fell from his horse.

Coll stared in disbelief as Gar turned to him, his face grim under the steel cap, his eyes burning.

Coll found his voice. "You slew a knight!"

"No," Gar told him. "He'll recover."

"But he's a knight!"

"So are we," Dirk reminded him.

"Oh." Coll blinked, gazing at the fallen knight, feeling very foolish indeed. "Yes, you are, aren't you?"

"And, after all," said Gar, "he *is* the enemy."

The door opened a crack, and four frightened eyes stared out. The younger two widened enormously at the sight of Gar.

Dirk drew up alongside Gar. "Who have you there?"

Coll turned in surprise, saw the open door and the wide young eyes that had swiveled to stare at Dirk, and pivoted back to tell his masters, "My family, sirs, or what's left of it— my mother and sister, all that I have."

"More than some men have." A shadow crossed Dirk's face. "But you can't stay here to guard them, Coll, which means they can't stay, either."

Coll's heart sank as he realized the truth of the knight's words. If he stayed until the battle was done, someone was bound to report him as an outlaw. He would be taken to the gibbet and hanged. If he left, though, his mother and sister might yet be prey for the soldiers.

Mama decided the issue for him. "He speaks truth, Coll, and we gathered our few belongings as soon as we heard the battle had started. We didn't get away in time, though. Come, Dicie! Say good-bye to your home, child, for there may not be anything left of it, if we ever come back."

Dicea stepped out the door, tears starting to her eyes; she stepped back and regarded the hut once, long and lingering, then turned to the future, looking up with wonder at the two stalwart knights who sat their horses above her. Coll stared at her face and felt a surge of relief—the eagerness with which she gazed at the men, the light that danced in her eyes, assured him that the knight had not come back for her after Coll had escaped. Perhaps he had been too busy with the hunt, and she so unimportant to him that he hadn't bothered to return.

"However did you make such friends as these, Coll?" Dicea breathed.

"Sheer luck," he grunted. "They saved me from an ambush before I had a chance to try to rob them."

Dirk laughed, and Gar smiled. "We had need of him, lass, for we are from far over the sea, and know little of your land. Your brother has, at least, given us enough knowledge to make it possible to find employment."

"As knights in the king's army?"

"The very same," Gar assured her, "and no one will be surprised if we disappear for a little while in the middle of a battle." He looked up at Coll. "Where shall we take them?"

"The greenwood, of course." Coll was amazed that the man could even ask the question. Surely the merest dolt could see that an outlaw had the choice of only two places where the lords' law didn't run: the forest or the wastelands, and the forest was much closer.

Or could it be that in their distant homeland, there were no places for outlaws to flee, and no need of them?

He put the thought behind him; it was too dizzying, too impossible. He reached down to take the heavy sack from his mother, but Gar said, "No. You may need your hands free to fight."

"I carried you for nine months, Coll," his mother assured him. "I can carry this sack for an hour."

Dicea regarded him merrily. "You wouldn't think twice about my hauling a basket of wet wash this heavy, but at the sight of a sack, you leap to carry."

"All right, haul your own blasted bag," Coll grunted, but he was secretly glad of the excuse. Gar was right; the clash of arms and the shouts of soldiers sounded all about them, mingled with the screams of serfs caught between the two forces. He ushered his mother and sister before him. The knights rode to either side, swords bare, shields high.

They came out from between the huts, and the fringe of battle caught them like a whirlwind. Coll backed up, facing away from his mother and sister, buffeting soldiers away with his buckler, taking quick glances behind to make sure he was still with the group. He saw Gar and Dirk hewing and thrusting with their swords, then turned back to see an earl's man rise up before him, eyes staring, mouth a gaping, fetid maw, the yell lost in the clamor all about them, swinging a halberd down at him one-handed—its pole had broken off short. Coll snapped his shield up and heard the halberd strike into it—then saw recognition start up in the man's eyes. Suddenly Coll knew him for Nud, the father of one of his childhood friends—but the battle whirled the two apart, and Coll fought on, fending off old companions and strangers, as the sinking feeling within him told him that the earl would learn that one of the king's soldiers was his escaped serf.

The battle boiled out of the village, whirling Coll and his protector-knights along with his family. Away and across the fields they went, until finally the ramparts of the forest rose up before them, and Coll and his family were swept in among the trees on a tide of relief. Dirk and Gar crowded in after them, and the giant called down, "Keep going! Work your way deeper and deeper into the greenwood, for this battle may yet invade the forest, and even if it doesn't, a lot of fleeing soldiers will!"

"They . . . saw me!" Coll turned to Gar in alarm. "Earl's soldiers, my fellow villagers, men from other villages who know me! They'll tell the earl!"

"I think Insol will have more weighty matters on his mind than an escaped serf," Dirk told him.

Gar nodded. "And even when he does have time to listen, no one will tell him, because the men who saw you will think they thought they saw something that wasn't there."

"But they recognized me! I saw it in their eyes!"

"Men see a lot of things in battle," Dirk assured him, "and not all of them are real."

Coll calmed, beginning to feel reassured. "Do you really think so?"

"Oh yes," Gar said with absolute certainty. "Be sure of it, Coll. Anybody who saw you will think they imagined it. Be sure."

Shouting and clanging sounded behind them, and the two knights turned to meet it, Dirk shouting, "Go!" Coll didn't stay to ask why, only turned to flee into the forest with his mother and sister.

An hour later, Mama stumbled over a tree root. Coll caught her arm; she looked up at him, and he saw her utter weariness. "We've gone far enough," he told her, and took the sack from her cramped fingers. "Let's find shelter."

They found it in a huge tree that had fallen against a smaller, lodging between a branch and the trunk; the younger tree held the older at an angle. Dead branches swept down to the ground, and Coll, forcing his way between them, found he was able to break off the ones inside, until he had a very serviceable lean-to. He brought the broken boughs out and Mama and Dicea in. Mama promptly lay down on the thick bed of fallen leaves and closed her eyes. Dicea brought out her coal box, then glanced at the trunk overhead and the dry boughs around them. "We can't light a fire in here, can we?"

"No, we'll have to go outside—but I think we'd better not light a fire at all," Coll answered. "Gar and Dirk seem to know the ways of war as well as anybody, and if they say fleeing soldiers may be coming through the wood, I wouldn't doubt them. They'll be hungry, looking for food and shelter, and I don't doubt they'll band together to take it.''

Dicea shuddered at the thought. ''We can make a cold meal.''

Suddenly, Coll realized he was hungry, raving hungry. ''Yes, Dicea, if you would! Even bread alone would be good!''

She reached into a bag, brought out a round loaf, passed it to Coll, then hefted a skin, unstoppered the foot, and held it out. Coll swallowed a mouthful of bread and squeezed a stream of liquid into his mouth. ''Ale! Bless you, Dicea!''

''Some breath of caution told me to bring it,'' she said, smiling. ''Now I see why—we may have to search for water.''

Coll nodded, carefully holding the foot of the aleskin upward. ''Only a few mouthfuls each, then—enough to make the bread go down, and no more.''

''Even so,'' Dicea agreed. She took the loaf back, broke off a third of it, and gave it back to Coll, then turned to Mama, saying softly, ''Mama, are you awake?''

''I only wish I weren't,'' Mama groaned. She forced herself up and took her third of the loaf. ''Still, you're right, child. I had better take nourishment while I can.''

They ate, finishing all of the loaf but only a quarter of the ale. Then Coll told them, ''Sleep while you can.''

''You must have rest too, though, son!'' his mother protested.

Coll nodded. ''I'll watch for four hours, then wake Dicea; she can watch and wake me if there's need. But I'll take the first watch, for I might not be able to stay awake for the second.''

''What sort of need are you expecting?'' Dicea asked, eyes wide.

''Those fleeing soldiers that Gar and Dirk spoke of,'' Coll told her. ''Odds are that, without a fire, we only need to sit still and let them pass us by—but I'd like to be awake when they come."

However, it wasn't runaway soldiers who found them as dusk closed in. Heavy hands suddenly wrenched the leaves of their lean-to aside, and a scarred, bearded face glared down at Coll, commanding, "Come out!"

Coll glared back at the man, taking in the leather jerkin, the grimy skin, and the dozen men behind him, all holding bows or quarterstaves, all wearing leather jerkins and leggins, all shaggy-haired and shaggy-bearded. With a sinking heart, he knew them for outlaws. "Come in and get me!" he snarled.

"As you'll have it, then." The outlaw glanced up and to the side, nodding, then turned a steady gaze on Coll.

Dry branches and leaves crashed; men shouted behind Coll in a sudden onslaught. Dicea and Mama screamed, and Coll whirled. The blow caught him on the back of the head, and he saw only a brief burst of stars before darkness took him.

Dicea's angry scream yanked him out of that darkness, and he scrambled to his feet—or tried to; something pulled hard on his arms behind his back, wrenching his shoulders with pain, and he fell back, sitting against something hard, curved, and rough. Pain throbbed through his head, and the light seemed far too bright, even though it couldn't have been all that much later. Fuzzy shapes became clear. He saw they were no longer in the lean-to, and he made out a couple of outlaws holding his mother, who strained against them, scolding. Two more were holding Dicea, and having a much tougher job restraining her arms—in fact, they were dancing back from her kicking feet, but another outlaw came up from behind to reach around and caress. "Scum!" Dicea shouted, and tried to turn to kick at the man, but he leaped back with a laugh.

"Scum and offal!" Coll shouted, and tried again to leap to Dicea's defense—but a hard pull yanked him back again, down hard, and he realized his wrists had been tied to a tree trunk, behind his back. Moreover, he realized that he was looking up at the outlaws; they had tied him sitting down. He gathered his legs under him and began to stand, turning from side to side in an awkward dance as he scraped the rope up the trunk.

But the biggest outlaw, the one who had commanded him to come out of the lean-to, put out a big hand and pushed him back. "I know it gripes you, lad, but we have need of women in the greenwood, and we're not about to let one pass by—especially one so pretty as this. She may have been your lady love, but . . ."

"She is my sister! And that woman's our mother!"

"Sister! And her mother watching?" The outlaw looked up at the women, dismayed, and Coll realized that he wasn't really a bad man, just a rather desperate one. Sure enough, his face hardened again, and he turned back to Coll. "Sister or not, we need her nonetheless. You've no choice, lad, for a runaway soldier has no place but the greenwood, and no people but . . ."

Coll surged at him with a roar of anger. To his amazement, his hands came up, fists balled. The outlaw froze in surprise, and Coll struck him down with a single blow. He caught up the man's spear and lunged at the outlaws holding Dicea. One of them dropped her hand with a shout and scrambled back, yanking his dagger free; Dicea whirled and slapped the other outlaw so hard the crack echoed through the trees. The man stepped back, dazed, and Dicea dove for the only cover available—the lean-to.

Coll whirled, striking with the spear butt at one of the men holding his mother. The man released her, but was too slow, and the wood cracked into his head. The other dropped Mama's hand and reached for his own dagger— and Coll grabbed Mama's wrist, pulling her, too, back into the lean-to.

"But what can we do here?" she cried.

"They have to come in to get us," Coll snarled, turning to guard the door hole.

Behind him, Dicea said, "This time, we'll be ready! Find a rock, Mama!"

Coll glanced at the ropes hanging from his wrists, unable to believe he had really broken them—and sure enough, the ends were clean, not frayed! But who could have cut them?

The outlaws were shouting outside, and he heard the clash of steel. Would they really kill him to get Dicea?

Yes. In an instant. He knew how badly the woman hunger had eaten at him, alone in the wilderness, and a girl as pretty as Dicea would make such a hunger much sharper. Coll knew these men would do anything to satisfy such lust. He leveled his spear.

"Do you think that pig-sticker will hold us off, boy?" the outlaw roared.

"I notice you're not making any move to come in," Coll retorted.

"There are half a dozen men on the other side of your shelter! Come out, or they'll come in at your back as I come in from the front!"

There was a rustle behind Coll, and Dicea hissed, "He lies!"

The outlaw glared, but his men were watching, so he beckoned them on and dove in after Coll with a roar.

Coll pushed his spear forward and grounded the butt. But the outlaw shoved it aside with contempt and seized Coll's neck in both hands. Coll rolled back, but managed to drive his knee up as the outlaw fell on him. It struck the outlaw's groin: his eyes went wide, and he made a gargling noise, but his hands only loosened a little, not enough for Coll to breathe. He rolled, trying to break the outlaw's hold, rolled him right next to Dicea—and his sister brained the outlaw with a rock.

Coll rolled free, gasping and choking, nodding thanks

to Dicea as he turned back to the hole, but two outlaws were already halfway through, grinning and stabbing at him with spears. Coll rolled aside, just enough so that both missed, and came up to strike a short, vicious jab into the nearest man's jaw. The other lunged for Dicea . . .

. . . and jolted to a stop so suddenly that his face slammed into the forest mold. Something dragged him backward. The other outlaw shouted as he turned to strike at whatever was at his feet. Coll drew his dagger, then set it against the man's throat. The outlaw froze, staring up at Coll, fear in his eyes.

The other outlaw shouted as whatever-it-was pulled him clear of the lean-to. There was a brief thrashing, a meaty thud, and he fell back into the door hole, limp and unconscious. Then the other bandit began to move, and Coll barely managed to twitch his knife aside in time. The man shouted as he slid out, and Coll stared after him, Dicea coming up beside him. They saw him sit up swinging a blow, saw Dirk let go of his ankles just in time to block and counterpunch right into the outlaw's jaw. The man swayed back, and Dicea struck with her rock again. He went limp. Dirk looked into the hole, eyebrows raised. "Maybe we should train *her* to the quarterstaff, Coll."

"Behind you!" the serf cried, and Dirk swung about to see a quarterstaff swinging at his head.

6

⟞⟋⟍⟋⟍⟋⟍⟋⟍⟋⟞

Dirk rolled, the quarterstaff gouged earth where he'd been, and he thrust upward. The outlaw dropped his staff with a howl, clutching his forearm; blood rose between his fingers. Dirk kept on rolling, up to his feet, and struck the man's head with the hilt of his sword. The outlaw fell like an ox in the shambles, and Dirk turned to the next enemy.

There was none, at least not nearby. Farther away, Gar was harrying a whole rank of outlaws, whooping and shouting as he rode from one end of the line to the other, then whirled his horse and rode back again, just in time to strike down the few who tried to slip past him to get at Coll and his family. Gar wasn't even using a sword—just a straight stick three feet long! Coll stared, amazed to realize the big man was actually having fun. He hadn't known Gar could.

"Coward!" the biggest outlaw raged. "Swine! Of course you can herd us all, with your steel shirt and your high horse and your sword at your hip! Come down from there and fight me man to man, if you've the heart for it!"

Gar drew in his horse, his eyes glittering.

"Oh, no!" Dirk groaned. "I never thought *he'd* be a sucker for a dare!" He stepped over to his own horse and mounted quickly.

Sure enough, Gar swung down from the saddle and un-buckled his breastplate. "I hope you fight as well as you talk, little man! I haven't had a good match in years!"

The "little man" was easily the biggest of the outlaws, more than six feet tall and burly as an oak. However he was still a head shorter than Gar, and although the knight looked less muscular, Coll had some idea of how strong he was. The outlaw stared at Gar, amazed to see him on the ground; then he grinned, showing several gaps between his stained teeth. "No match in years? Then you're out of prac-tice, I'd say."

"Come on and find out," Gar invited.

The big outlaw saw that Gar's hands were still busy with buckles; he roared and charged, flailing with his sword. Gar stepped inside the swing, caught his arm, and whirled, send-ing the big outlaw flying. As he fell, the giant called, "You'll have to do better than that!"

The outlaw scrambled to his feet. "Hang all knights and their fancy tricks!"

"Try." Gar tossed his breastplate aside. "Just try."

The outlaw bellowed and charged again, arms wide for a bear hug. Gar yanked off his helmet and threw it in the man's face. "I'm not done disrobing, if you don't mind."

The big outlaw went reeling back; two of his men stepped forward to catch him. He threw them off with a snarl and went to pick up his sword as Gar pulled the chain-mail shirt over his head and threw it over his horse's withers. "I like to know who I'm fighting. Do you have a name?"

The outlaw chief reddened. "Aye, I've a name, and a proper one it is! I'm Banhael, I am! What are you? And no 'sir,' mind you—I said man to man!"

"Well enough. I'm Gar." Banhael gave a shout of de-light, and the giant grinned. "Yes, only one syllable—a name fit for a serf. You've two syllables, so you feel your name is distinguished, I take it."

Banhael wasn't too sure what a syllable was, but he knew a mocking tone when he heard one. "We'll see which of us fights like a peasant," he growled, "and which like a knight!" With that, he leaped forward, slashing with his two-handed sword, not even pausing to riposte but slashing again from the other side, over and over again in a rough figure eight.

He managed it so easily because Gar didn't stop to block a single cut; he only retreated, smiling as though he were amused. That angered Banhael. His sword swings became wilder and wilder as he roared, "Stand still, you hopping monkey! Stand and fight!"

"If you say so," Gar said agreeably, and brought his own sword up in a parry. Banhael's blade glanced off it and shot into the dirt. He yanked it out with a curse—and felt a wasp sting on his neck. The other outlaws called out angrily as he clapped a hand to it, a hand that came away with a smear of blood of a color that matched the smear on the end of Gar's blade. "Count your throat cut," Gar said quietly, "but like a true hero, fight on until I've stabbed your heart."

"You would, would you!" Banhael shouted, and swung a huge, vicious overhand chop straight at Gar's head.

Of course, that head wasn't there when the blow landed. Gar danced aside, then in to catch Banhael's wrist as his sword sank into the dirt again. He tried to draw it out, but Gar held his wrist down as he stepped up chest to chest, gazing down into the shorter man's face and purring, "I should think you'd have learned not to swing that cleaver as though you were chopping logs. You should try thrusting with the point, like this." He leaped back, his rapier flickered in, and Banhael felt a sting on his cheek. "Second blood," Gar said quietly. "Do try thrusting, Banhael."

"Just as you say, teacher," Banhael snarled, and stabbed two-handed, straight toward Gar's chest.

Gar parried; the sword hissed aside, cutting the cloth of his gambeson. Redness stained the padding, and the bandits shouted approval. "There," Gar said. "See how much more effective it is? But your technique is faulty; you should thrust like this!" The rapier flickered in again, feinting quickly toward hip, then toward heart; in a panic, Banhael swung his huge blade from side to side, but the rapier was gone before his crude block arrived, then darted in a third time to score his other cheek. The outlaws shouted in anger, and Coll gathered himself to charge out to protect his friend if they mobbed him—and hoped his friend could protect Coll and his family. The outlaws did start toward the duelers—but Dirk moved his horse halfway around the little clearing, and they ground to a halt, watching him warily. His own rapier was drawn now, and he, too, was grinning.

Banhael turned crafty then. He circled Gar, huge sword weaving, seeking an opening. Gar circled around his circle, grinning, then obligingly dropped his guard. "Hah!" Banhael shouted in glee, and lunged. But Gar's sword leaped back up, and Banhael saw to his horror that he was hurtling straight toward its point. He tried to stop in midair, to twist aside—and Gar's blade circled the outlaw's sword, catching it and flinging it away. Then Gar stepped in, striking with his sword hilt, and Banhael, off balance, fell. He pushed himself up—and found himself staring at the tip of Gar's sword.

"A man once told me that, from this position, all you can look forward to is a quick surrender or a quicker death," Gar said pleasantly. "Which do you choose?"

The outlaws shouted and started forward—and Dirk's horse leaped out along their line, his sword swinging in circles just in front of the bandits' noses. Sharp cracks echoed as his blade cut the heads off a couple of spears, and the men crowded backward.

"I surrender," Banhael croaked.

"Well, let me see," Gar mused. "Shall I let you live? Accept your surrender? I think there should be a price for my self-denial—a night's lodging, let us say, and a good supper of roast meat."

Banhael glared at him, but he was glaring up along the length of Gar's rapier, so he forced himself to say, choking on every word, "Of course. Be our guests. We will be delighted to give you our finest guest hut and our choicest cuts."

"Of meat, I hope you mean. Well, thank you! We accept your hospitality." Gar withdrew his sword and held down a hand. Banhael took it and clambered to his feet. "I don't think I need to tell you what will happen if you're foolish enough to try to betray us," Gar said with a slight smile.

Banhael looked into his eyes and shuddered. "Breach hospitality? We wouldn't think of it!"

"Oh, yes you would," Dirk called.

Banhael reddened. "Well, we would never *do* anything about it. Your persons shall be sacred, sir knights, as shall those of these folk you've so strangely fought to protect."

"Not so strange as all that," Gar told him. "Coll is our squire, and these women are his mother and sister."

"Yes, we've had the pleasure of meeting," Banhael said dryly. "Well, come along, then." He turned to bark orders to his men, and they set off through the forest.

"Not quite so quickly, if you please," Gar said with an edge to his voice, "and I'd appreciate it if you'd choose a pathway more suited to horses."

The outlaws slowed, and Banhael glanced back at him, glowering. "Well, come along, then!"

"Quickly, you three," Gar said softly.

Coll led his mother and sister scrambling out from their

lean-to, then fell behind them as they hurried after the bandits. He looked up at Gar. "The outlaws' camp is anything
but the place we want to go."

"You've nothing to fear, with the two of us beside you,"
Gar assured him.

Dirk explained, "Gar beat Banhael in a fair fight. That
took the boss outlaw down in his band's view, which means
they could turn on him. He has to boost himself back up,
and the easiest way to do that is to chum up to Gar."

Coll gave him a wary glance. "What's the harder way?"

"To ambush us," Gar told him, "killing us in our sleep,
for example. But he knows he could get killed that way, and
so do his men."

Dirk nodded. "We're not fools enough to sleep without
leaving someone on watch, and he knows it."

"How?"

"If none of Earl Insol's soldiers have fled to Banhael's
band yet," Gar said, "they will soon—and they'll carry rumors about the two stranger knights who led the king's
forces."

Coll looked up in alarm. "Earl Insol lost, then?"

"Oh yes," Gar assured him, "and the king won, easily."

"If you don't count the number of peasant soldiers dead
on the battlefield," Dirk said grimly, "and the number of
serfs who got trampled underfoot."

Gar shrugged. "When have these aristocrats ever
counted any body that wasn't encased in armor?"

A vision of men of his own village lying dead and bleeding flashed before Coll's eyes. Grief swamped him, then
yielded to the slow anger that began to burn inside him
again.

"Grieve, then let it pass as a river flows past a ford," Gar
said softly. "Then perhaps we can find some way to end this
ceaseless fighting, and the deaths that go with it."

"Be glad none of the dead are your own this time," Dirk
said, equally softly.

Coll nodded, letting the anger push the grief aside until there would be time to deal with it—and until he was sure it was warranted; he hadn't actually *seen* any dead men he had known yet. "But won't the king be angry when you don't come back?"

"His Majesty may regret losing two such useful knights," Gar acknowledged, "but men are always disappearing in battle, especially when they refuse to wear full armor. When we do come back, he will be delighted that we have escaped the enemy, or found our way out of the swamps, and won't ask too closely why it took us so long."

"There are advantages to being useful," Dirk agreed.

The outlaws' camp surprised them all. It was a regular village, hidden deep within the greenwood, surrounded by trunks and roofed over by leafy boughs. Men went about their tasks—fletching arrows, skinning game, thatching roofs, practicing archery. A few children ran here and there in some frantic game, and there and here, a woman stirred a pot or roasted a fowl over a fire.

"Ah!" Mama cried. "Decent cooking!" And she bustled Dicea off to the nearest campfire, to chatter merrily with the woman there. The cook looked up in surprise, then smiled and answered a question. In minutes, they were all laughing and gossiping.

Banhael shook his head in wonder. "Women! Total strangers, and they're god-sibs in five minutes!"

"My mother has a way of making friends," Coll told him.

"She does indeed!"

"You do seem to have quite a few women," Gar pointed out, looking about the camp. "Why were you so desperate to find more?"

"Because all my men want them, but only one out of five has one," Banhael answered shortly. "There's constant fighting over it. I could almost wish for a priest to come and set some marriages, so my men would know which women were taken and not to be stolen away!"

"*Your* men?" Gar turned back to him. "Are you the leader of this whole motley crew, then?"

"I am," Banhael answered, with a level, defiant glare.

"How fortunate," Gar said mildly. "Then I won't have to fight twice."

"Would you dare?" Banhael demanded. "I've four times as many men around me now!"

"The ones you had didn't do you much good before," Gar pointed out.

Banhael glared at him, but something distracted him— maybe the rattle as Dirk loosened his rapier in its scabbard—and he turned away with a snarl.

"Where is this guest's hut you told us about?" Dirk asked.

"Come along, I'll show you," Banhael grunted. "Such *honored* guests should be led by the captain himself!"

He took them to a hut that was almost identical to all the others. Dirk ducked inside while Gar strolled around the outside, inspecting. "Needs a bit of new thatch, doesn't it?"

"You're welcome to make it better any way you want," Banhael grunted. "Not much need to worry about the roof, though—there's no sign of rain tonight."

"True, but we might want to stay a few days." Gar waited just long enough to see dismay register on Banhael's face, then turned to Dirk, who was coming out the door. "How is it?"

"Needs sweeping," Dirk informed him, "and we might want to shovel the ashes out of the hearth, in case we're here long enough for the weather to turn cold."

"But it's summer!" Banhael protested.

"I like to plan ahead," Gar informed him. "I believe there was some mention of dinner?"

"Cook it yourself!" Banhael snapped, and turned away.

Gar watched him go, amused. "How soon do you think he'll gather his men to attack us?"

"Tomorrow night," Dirk said immediately. "I think he'll let us be for tonight, and hope we'll go away all by ourselves."

"That might not be a bad idea." Coll glanced nervously around the camp, his gaze returning to his sister and mother.

"There is some merit to the notion," Gar admitted, "but we do want to give the losing soldiers time to sneak home, and get out of our way."

"On the other hand," Dirk reminded him, "we don't want to be gone *too* long, or the king will think we've been up to something."

"Why not give him grounds for concern?" Gar mused. "Besides, we might not choose to go back to him."

"You're not thinking of *staying* in this den of thieves!" Coll protested.

"No," Gar admitted, "but there are other possibilities . . . I see these outlaw women, at least, are generous."

Coll turned, and saw Mama and Dicea coming up laden with food: Dicea carried a small kettle. "How hospitable they are!" Mama exclaimed. "I've two new recipes to try out right away! And it was so good of Pinella to lend us her spare pot!"

Coll stared, and Gar shook his head, marveling. "You forage amazingly, goodwife."

For a moment, a tinge of sadness showed. "Call me 'goodwife' no longer, sir—no, not since my husband died in the earl's wars, God rest his soul. Call me 'mother,' or 'widow.' " Then she brightened. "But for now, call me 'cook'! Come, Dicea, I see a hearth of stones! Kindle a fire and set up the tripod!"

"I can do that much, at least." Coll gathered up some dry grass and a few sticks and settled down with flint and steel.

Mama gazed down at him fondly. "He's a good boy, sir. On the headstrong side, yes, and he does have a temper, but he's a good boy."

"We've found him so," Gar agreed. "You've made friends quickly enough, Mother."

"Oh, they're so kindly, sir! Even eager, I might say, for the company of an older woman! They've been reft from their mothers, you see—from their villages, for that matter, all of them, or so Pinella tells me."

"Does she really?" Gar said, with keen interest—almost admiration, it seemed to Coll. "I would have thought they were outlaws themselves."

"Well, some of them are, sir. They fled to the forest rather than go to the bed of a cruel knight, then found themselves bundled into the blankets of a bandit instead." Mama saddened a little. "Some fled because they were charged with stealing, and would rather take their chances with wild beasts than lose a hand—but I don't know as they thought of the beasts who went on two legs. Indeed, some of them are girls who were foolish enough to venture into the woods alone, and were stolen away to be an outlaw's consort whether they would or no."

"Foolish indeed." But Dicea sounded angry.

"I thought everybody knew about the outlaws in the forest," Dirk said, and Gar shot him a curious glance.

"All do, sir, all do," Mama sighed, "but young girls never think they might be as hard as the knights or their soldiers. Still, men are men, and what can a woman do with them?"

"Try to tame them, of course," Gar said, and Mama looked up in surprise. "Why, so they do, sir, though I never thought to hear a man admit it! But even as you say, some of the women have settled down with one man only, borne him children, and become wives in all but name—and in that too! Though without a priest to bless the union, other men keep challenging their husband's right."

"And if he's a bad husband, she's tempted to change partners," Dirk said dryly. "That's where you get the really nasty fights."

"True, sir, though there's always fighting over the women who haven't yet managed to get a man to themselves."

"Let me guess," Dirk said. "It's the prettiest ones who have managed the common-law marriages."

Mama frowned. "An odd term, sir, though I doubt not it will serve—if there were a law common to all serfs, not set upon them by their lords. Yet you guess wrongly, for it isn't the most beautiful women who wed. Indeed, many here are beauties, or they would not have needed to flee the lords, but what cares a man about beauty, when there are so few women?"

Dirk nodded. "Nice if you can get it, but not exactly vital. So what does determine who gets married?"

Mama shrugged. "Those who make a man most yearn for them, sir—by their conduct, I suppose, though I notice the 'wives' are the older women."

"Yes, must be well into their twenties," Dirk sighed. "Y'know, Gar, the whole setup seems very familiar."

"Familiar?" Mama frowned, looking from one knight to the other. "How so?"

"Like an outlaw band he knew at home, I think," Gar explained, "and so did I."

" 'Home' for these gentlemen was very far away, Mama," Coll explained.

"Very," Dirk agreed, his voice flat. "But there was a band there that we spent some time with, whose captain was a woman."

"A woman?" Mama stared. "Captain of an outlaw band? How could she make her men mind?"

"By sheer force of personality," Gar told her, "coupled with an unfailingly fair and accurate sense of judgment, and very high intelligence."

"Even so, I marvel that a woman could rise to rule men!"

"She was a very exceptional woman," Gar agreed, "and would have been so in any society, anywhere."

"Did she not bend men by power of beauty?" Dicea asked.

"No, because she didn't have any," Dirk answered. "She was plain, and very fat. They called her 'Lapin,' which means 'rabbit,' because she taught her men to run and hide from the lords' men when they didn't stand an even chance of winning."

"Wise advice," Coll grunted.

"Yes, wasn't it? So her band survived and grew, while the others were killed off. After a few years, she virtually ruled the forest."

"I don't see any such wisdom in Banhael." Coll frowned at the outlaw leader, who was cuffing one of his men, then roaring an order.

"No, so I've no doubt he'll only last until someone smarter comes along," Gar said. "But he's a good fighter, and canny in his ambushes, as you've found out all too well, so his band has grown and lasted long enough for some of the men to marry and start families."

Coll pursed his lips, frowning. "So as long as he wins and keeps them alive, they'll listen to him?"

Gar nodded. "The real test of an outlaw leader, I suppose—simple survival."

"Yes, and survival is what being an outlaw is all about," Gar agreed. "In fact, if you have oppressive lords with unfair laws, and punishments so harsh that a man has less to lose by fleeing and hiding than by submitting to punishment, it's inevitable that you'll have outlaws in the forest."

"Yes, provided that you have forests so big they're impossible to police," Dirk said.

Gar nodded. "Or mountains so high and rugged that

any army going in will be cut down man by man before they
can fight a pitched battle—or deserts or glaciers where a
man who knows the territory can outlast any soldier. Yes, I
daresay outlaw bands are inevitable indeed.''

"But having a leader like Lapin, who did what Lapin
did, is anything but sure," Dirk said somberly.

"Why, what did Lapin do?" Mama asked brightly.

Dirk glanced at Gar, who stood immobile a moment,
then gave a cautious nod. Dirk sighed and turned back to
Mama. "Lapin led her bandits in a revolt against the lords,"
he said, "at the same time that a dozen other bands rose
up."

Dicea gasped; Coll stared, feeling the hair rise on the
nape of his neck; and Mama quavered, "How slowly did she
die?"

"Not at all," Dirk answered. "In fact, she's still alive, and
doing quite well, thank you. She's the head of all the rebels,
and they're the government of the plan . . . uh, kingdom,
now.''

"But what of the lords?" Dicea asked, eyes round.

"There were a few good ones," Dirk admitted. "The
rest are dead."

Coll's head swam with the audacity, the enormity of it!
Serfs overthrow the lords? No, impossible! Surely impossible!

But if it weren't . . .

"A deed of heroes!" Mama breathed, and Dicea echoed
her. "Was this in an age of legend, sir?"

"Well, no, actually," Dirk said, shifting uncomfortably.
"It was six months ago. But far away, mind you! Very far
away! And the rebels had a lot of help, from a wizard."

"Two wizards," Gar muttered, "one of whom *was* a legend."

Dirk shot him a dark look. "But one of whom was very
much alive."

"Yes, he was, wasn't he?" Gar stared straight at Dirk.

"You aren't thinking what I think you're thinking," Dirk said, his voice hollow.

"Oh, but I am," Gar said softly.

7

G ar began work on Banhael during dinner that very
night. The outlaws had roasted a deer, and everyone
sat around the center of the encampment, sharing the meat
and whatever roots, nuts, and berries the women had gathered.

"Are all your meals like this?" Gar asked. "The whole
band eating together, I mean."

"Dinner, yes," Banhael grunted. "Otherwise, it's up to
each man to find what he can. Those with women fare better than single men."

"Yes, women do seem to make life better, if they care
enough to do more than warm a man's bed," Gar reflected.
"In fact, I'm surprised to find your band so well established
that you *can* have women."

Banhael took the left-handed compliment with another
grunt, but he puffed himself up a little. "We're the largest
band in the forest, sir knight, and we're hidden deep, with
sentries always on watch. Yes, my men can offer a woman
safety, and some assurance of a good future."

"Yes, as long as the game stays plentiful," Gar mused,
"and the other bands don't join together against you."

Banhael looked up, startled. "Why should they do that?"

"To make sure you won't attack any one of them," Gar returned. "That's why you started building your band, wasn't it?"

Banhael turned away to frown at the fire. "I suppose it was, now that you mention it—'join up or die.' "

Gar nodded. "Very much the sort of thing, yes. After all, what's the surest way to guarantee that someone else doesn't attack you?"

"Attack him first," Banhael grunted. "I guess it is pretty clear, isn't it?"

"Paranoid, too," Dirk muttered, but Gar went on easily. "Very clear. In fact, I suspect that's how the first lords came to power."

"The lords? Attack first? 'Join or die'?" Banhael looked up in surprise, then turned thoughtful, nodding slowly. "Yes, that makes sense. I'd always thought they were born lords right from the first."

"That's what they want you to believe," Dirk said with a cynical smile.

Gar nodded. "Every noble house began with a man who *wasn't* born to power, but seized it by force of arms."

"Well, I suppose knights should know." Banhael still sounded doubtful.

"But not too well, you mean?" Gar gave him a sardonic smile. "If we really understood it, we would seize power for ourselves?"

"Of course, it *could* be that's exactly what we're doing," Dirk pointed out, "only you're seeing us when we're just starting out."

"And need a small army of your own to begin with, eh? Such as a band of outlaws in a forest? Do you think I've made myself a little army just so you can take it and use it?" Banhael demanded.

Gar nodded approval. "You do understand us, don't you?"

Yes, Banhael understood them, Coll realized—as long as they led him to it, step by step.

"I've no lust for cleared lands and tilled fields," Banhael snapped. "The greenwood is enough for me,"

"Yes, but how *much* of it?" Gar demanded.

There was a shout; they looked up as a drum began to beat, and one of the younger women began to move her feet in time to it. A young man stepped out to join her, then another, and older outlaws took up instruments, one a willow pipe, another a sort of fiddle.

"Enough of this talk of armies and lords." Banhael turned to watch the dancers with glittering eyes. "Life is for pleasure."

"True," Gar agreed, "though sometimes you have to fight hard to have anything to enjoy."

"Or work hard to gather or raise it," Dirk pointed out.

Coll felt a rush of gratitude—all this talk of armies and fighting was making him nervous. Hadn't Gar and Dirk said that was what they wanted to stop?

They certainly seemed to have forgotten it for the time being. Gar was clapping his hands in time to the beat, and Dirk was stepping out to join the dancers. With a gleam in her eye, Dicea rose to join them, and the rest of the evening was spent in revelry—and, for Coll, in worry, for he knew his sister was doomed to disappointment. Dirk didn't have the look of a man who was ready to settle down—not yet, nor for a long time to come. Neither did Gar, for that matter— and it did matter, since Coll had seen her eyeing the bigger knight, too. In fact, there was a quality of aloofness about Gar that belied the friendliness and occasional warmth of his words, a sense of standing back and watching the life that went on about him without really being part of it. Nonsense, of course, considering the number of fights Coll had seen Gar embroiled in, or the fact that he had led Dirk in rescuing Coll himself—or the battle they had just won, which Gar had virtually commanded. Yes, it was nonsense, but the feeling was there nonetheless.

Banhael brought up the issue himself over breakfast, or what passed for it—black bread and cheese, washed down with warm ale. "Look you," he said truculently, "it's plain flat impossible to fight the lords. I know, for two years ago, I gathered fifty men who were eager for revenge and came out of the woodland to seize a village. The lord led his knights and men-at-arms against us and killed half my men outright. The other half were lucky to escape to the greenwood, and it was two years and four victories over smaller bands before they had any faith in me again."

Coll didn't like the sound of that. Trying to seize a village? Why, Banhael was no better than the lords themselves—or, he realized with a shock, the lords were no better than Banhael, and wasn't that what Gar had been saying last night?

No, he had been saying a bit more, at least to judge by the way he was nodding at Banhael's words and the earnest attention he gave the bandit chief. "So you had the courage to try! But what are fifty archers and quarterstaff men against armored knights and soldiers with halberds? How many of them were there—a hundred to your fifty? Two hundred?"

"Twice our number at least," Banhael grunted, "but what does that matter? A lord will always have more soldiers at his call than I will have bandits, and trained warriors, too, every one of them!"

"Then train your men," Gar retorted. "I can see they're skilled archers already. How many bands are there in this forest? A dozen? A score?"

"Only two or three like ours," Banhael countered,

"large enough to build huts and care for children. But there are sixteen others that I know of, though most are only half a dozen men who scrabble for a living."

"Perhaps two hundred men in all," Gar summarized. "And there are a dozen forests in this land of yours . . ."

"Twelve?" Banhael looked up, startled.

"Fourteen, actually," Dirk told him.

Coll stared. How did two men from so far away, who were so ignorant of this land in every other way, know what even he himself didn't? And so sure of it, too!

"If there are as many men in each of those forests as there are here," Gar told him, "you'll have twenty-five hundred men and more. Not a great number, no, but enough to win a few battles, if you fight like outlaws, not soldiers."

"Like outlaws?" Banhael scowled. "How do you mean?"

"Soldiers fight by lining up in an open field, then charging at each other. Outlaws fight by leaping out from behind trees, striking a blow or loosing an arrow, then leaping back."

"Oh, that way!" Banhael said in surprise. "Well, of course. But how do you hide behind a tree in an open field?"

"You find what you can—a ditch, a barn, a bush, or even bring some greenery with you. But why should you fight in a field?"

"Because that's where the soldiers are!"

Gar shook his head. "Let them stand there alone all day, while you wait for them among the trees. If you wait long enough, they'll either go away or come in after you."

"Why, so they will, won't they?" Banhael said, wide-eyed. "But what good does that do if you're trying to take a village from its lord?"

"There, you send the villagers to the forest, and have your men hide behind the huts—or hide in the forest yourselves, and chop the soldiers to bits when they come in after you. *Then* you take the village."

Banhael guffawed, slapping his knee. "You have an answer for everything, don't you? But how can an outlaw fight a soldier, man to man, and win, eh? The soldier is trained to it!"

"As I've already told you." Gar spread his hands. "Train your men as well."

"Easy to say." Banhael scowled. "How do you do it?"

"Let me show you." Gar rose and stepped out into the center of the village clearing. "Bring me a dozen men."

Banhael smiled, wide and wolfish. "Wawn! Brock! Lod! Ang! Bring each three men with you, and go to Sir Gar there."

Coll stared as the men lined up facing one another as Gar gave them directions. Did the giant really know what he was doing, know what pack of hounds he was unleashing? Coll didn't doubt for a minute that Banhael would take all Earl Insol's lands if he could—and everything considered, Coll wasn't all that sure that he wouldn't rather be ruled by Earl Insol than by Banhael.

Lord Banhael? He shuddered at the thought, and watched Gar's fighting lessons with misgiving. He was teaching them to use quarterstaves as spears, Coll saw, and knew that soon enough, these expert staff fighters would be the equal of any soldier who knew a spear only as a stabbing weapon. If Gar went on to teach them how to use their swords properly, could this ragtag batch of escaped serfs really challenge a lord's army and win?

Yes, if the army weren't too big. But the lords had far more soldiers than the forests had outlaws, even if all the bandits *could* be made to obey one single lord. Coll relaxed. Training these outlaws might make trouble for the lords on their own estates, but would scarcely overthrow them.

Why, then, was Gar training them?

Then Coll noticed that he wasn't the only one watching the training. The other outlaws were gathering around, watching the session with keen interest . . .

. . . and so was Dicea.

She sat a short distance away from Coll, watching the training with shining eyes—no, Coll saw, watching Gar! He looked again at her face, the glowing smile, the fluttering lashes, and felt his heart sinking deeper. He tried to console himself with the notion that if she was smitten with both Gar and Dirk, she couldn't be interested enough in either one to be terribly hurt—but it really wasn't much comfort at all; he loved his sister dearly, but he didn't doubt for a minute that she was quite capable of being in love with two men at the same time—or, well, not with the men, exactly, so much as with the idea of being a knight's lady.

If she was, she was doomed to disappointment. Coll gazed at his sister, feeling his heart twist, and hoped that she could learn to guard her feelings as well as the outlaws were learning to guard their bodies.

Coll had known it would be inevitable that Gar would call upon him to demonstrate his combined spear-and-quarter-staff skills, then put him to work helping train the men in the new sort of unarmed combat he was teaching them, where feet counted for as much as fists, and open hands chopped like hatchets. In particular, Coll had learned how to shift from punching to wrestling with the tricks Dirk had shown him, and he was far enough ahead of the outlaws to do some real teaching. After two days, Coll was amazed at the outlaws' change in attitude. The women had taken Mama and Dicea to their hearts from the first, of course, but the men began to be friendly with Coll, chatting and inviting him to practice his archery with them. They were impressed by his skill there, too, and by the second day, they were joking and gossiping with him as though they were old friends.

Still, they made no attempt to hide the lustful glances they gave Dicea, and Coll knew better than to try to stop her from flirting with every man in sight—it seemed as natural to her as breathing, and he wasn't always sure she knew she was doing it. These woman-hungry lust buckets didn't understand that, though, and Coll braced himself for the fight he knew was coming.

Before it did, he found he was going.

On the morning of the third day, Gar declared, "They know enough now to pull themselves together, and draw in more bands."

"Read: take over," Dirk said.

Gar shrugged. "Banhael's band already has enough reputation to pull in recruits of their own accord, especially when winter comes. The next convoy a lord sends through the forest will never reach its destination, and Banhael's band will grow in reputation. The other bands may not join up, but they'll do what he says."

"Is this truly a good thing?" Coll asked.

"Good enough for our purposes," Gar said, but didn't explain. "Time for us to move along and spread the word that the lords can be beaten."

"But isn't that a lie?" Coll protested.

"Oh, no," Dirk said softly. "Be very sure, it's not a lie."

"But there aren't enough outlaws to fight all those soldiers!"

"There are, when you consider that most of the soldiers spend most of their time fighting one another," Dirk pointed out. "Besides, outlaws aren't the only ones who can fight."

"Who, then?" Coll said, completely at a loss.

"Let's go find out, shall we?" Gar said quietly. "Or would you prefer to stay here, with the outlaws?"

"Don't feel you *have* to come," Dirk said quickly. "I won't lie—we'd much rather have you with us—but we'll understand if you want to stay. It is more secure than the open road, after all."

Coll agreed with that, but he saw a big, burly outlaw, one

of the ones who shaved once a week and bathed once a
month, pausing to eye Dicea as she moved about the cooking fire, and since Gar and Dirk were watching, she was at
her most graceful. "I would like to," he said slowly, "but my
mother and sister may not, and I can't leave them alone
again."

"Of course not," Gar agreed. He turned to the women.
"Will you come with us, Mother, lass?"

"Ah, me!" Mama sighed. "It would indeed be pleasant
to stay in the greenwood, and I would certainly feel quite
safe myself—but Dicea . . ."

"Don't you dare leave me here!" Dicea exclaimed.
"There isn't a man among them who hasn't been undress-
ing me with his eyes, and with you gone, they wouldn't hesitate a minute to do it with their hands!" She glanced at the
two knights out of the corner of her eye as she said it.

Coll glanced, too, and saw Gar only nodding judiciously.
Dirk said, "No, you'd better come with us."

"We will certainly be glad of your company," Gar said.
"Coll's advice has been invaluable, and the presence of
women always sweetens the day."

Dicea blushed and lowered her eyes, and even Mama
flushed with pleasure. Coll wondered if the big knight knew
that what he intended as mere gallantry, Dicea might take
as flirtation.

So that afternoon, they bade good-bye to Banhael and
his men. The leader was quite surprised, and tried to talk
them into staying. "You will be welcome, you will be more
than welcome!" He shot a covetous glance at Dicea, and
Coll could have killed the old goat—he had a woman and
three cubs at home! "You don't need to worry about attack,
Sir Gar . . ."

"I know." Gar clapped Banhael on the shoulder. "I've
come to trust you amazingly in just these two days, Banhael."

Which meant that it would be amazing if he trusted Banhael at all, Coll thought. On the other hand, *he* could trust Banhael, too—trust him to try to bundle Dicea into his bed the moment her brother and the two knights were out of sight. Come to think of it, Gar could trust Banhael quite a lot, indeed—trust him to stick a knife in his back as soon as he didn't need Gar anymore, trust him to betray the knights at every turn, trust him to try to twist the knights' presence into a way of gaining mastery over the forest, then over the wider world . . .

"But there are other forests we must visit, other bands we must tell about you and your resolve," Gar explained.

Banhael covered a quick look of alarm; he had planned to be the bandit leader to control all the forests. However, Gar's second phrase seemed to reassure him—a little.

"We have to go looking for other groups of men who want to stop the lords' oppression," Dirk explained. "If it all comes down to numbers, we've got to dredge them up."

Gar nodded. "There are more serfs than lords, after all. There must be some way to arm and raise more of them than the lords can."

Banhael looked skeptical, but all he said was, "Well, if I can't dissuade you, then I can wish you well. Vinal! Oram! Guide these guests out of the forest by the most secret path!"

So they set off out of the settlement with Banhael's parting gift—another stallion and two ponies, for the women to ride.

And, of course, his guides to follow. Coll rode with his spear in his fist, and noticed that Gar and Dirk each kept a hand close to his sword. In spite of it all, though, they rode unthreatened to the edge of the forest, where Vinal and Oram touched their forelocks and Vinal said, "Yonder lies the pastureland and the plowed fields, sir knights."

"We wish you well, and so does Banhael," Oram said. "Remember, if things go wrong out there, you'll always have friends and a home in here."

Coll hoped they wouldn't have to live in it.

They wouldn't, at least for the moment. As the afternoon waned into twilight, they came upon a ragtag band of people clustered around a campfire, backed by two oxcarts. They looked up warily as Gar and Dirk rode up, but some of the women glanced behind the knights and saw two peasant women, which seemed to reassure them somewhat. The oldest man, a hale and hearty greybeard, stood and came toward them, sweeping off his hat to bow. "Good evening, good sirs! Can a poor band of mountebanks aid you in any way?"

"Mountebanks!" Gar and Dirk exchanged a startled glance, then turned back to the man with slow smiles. "Are you players?" Dirk asked.

"We have that privilege, sir."

"Actors who perform plays?" Gar clarified.

"Well, we do try," the man said with a self-effacing smile.

"Then we would like to travel with you to your next performance, so that we may watch," Gar told him. "Would that trouble you?"

"No-no, not at all," the man said, with a look that verged on panic. The other players stirred uneasily, trying to hide their alarm.

"Oh, yes it does," Dirk said with a smile. "We'll camp near you, then, but not with you, and follow you in the morning." He turned his horse away, and Coll turned with him—but his gaze lingered on one young woman, a red-headed, sloe-eyed beauty, who noticed his interest and lost her alarm in a slow, measuring smile.

Dicea frowned and moved her pony forward. "Then let us find a resting place quickly, while there is still light."

"Yes, of course!" Dirk jolted himself out of his reverie. "We'll see you in the morning then, players."

"Good night to you, sir knights," the greybeard said, obviously relieved, and the party moved on—but Coll glanced back twice, and felt his heart leap when he saw that the red-head's gaze stayed fixed on him.

Gar pulled them off the road into a small clearing. The earth was beaten hard, and there were two rings of blackened stones with the evidence of many fires. "This seems to be a virtual way station. Did you bring canvas, Dirk?"

"Canvas? Sure." Dirk dismounted and pulled a thick square of folded cloth from a saddlebag. So did Gar. They pitched camp, and Mama set herself to working wonders with dried meat, some roots that she grubbed up, and a kettleful of water. Scarcely had she set the pot over the fire, though, when she exclaimed with annoyance, "Savory! There's none to be found. I'll just walk back to those players, and see if they have any."

"You shouldn't go alone, Mama," Coll said quickly. "I'll go with you." He fell in beside his mother, his heartbeat quickening at the thought of red hair and huge eyes. He heard scraps of talk behind him.

"Now, why would the good widow do that?" Gar wondered. "Surely the herbs cannot be so very important!"

Dicea turned to him, forcing a smile that became real as she gazed at him. "It isn't the savory she really goes for, sir—it's the other travelers."

"Oh, of course." Gar nodded. "I expect the company of other women would be comforting. Are you sure you don't want to go with her?"

Dicea gazed up at him, and her eyelids drooped. "By your leave, sir, I'd sooner stay here with yourself and Sir Dirk."

Coll frowned, a little nettled at not being even an afterthought, which he always had been, as far as Dicea was concerned. He sighed, glad that he wasn't going to have to stay to watch his sister flirt with the impassive giant.

8

Mama and Coll came back in less than an hour, Mama wreathed in smiles, Coll with a slight curve to his lips and a strange light to his eyes that made Dicea frown. He had just had fifteen minutes' talk with the most beautiful creature he had ever seen, and felt as though his blood were wine.

"Oh, what hospitable folk they are!" Mama held up a bunch of greenery. "Dried savory, and rosemary and sage, too!"

"And good conversation with it?" Gar asked, smiling.

"A great deal of news." Mama sat down beside the kettle and crumbled a little savory into the stewing meat. "There, now, half an hour more, and your dried meat and vegetables should have turned into a most appetizing stew. Such good conversation, my! They've heard of the battle already, how the king fought with Earl Insol, and won—and without even slaying all that many men, though a good number are lost on both sides."

"Lost or slain, what difference?" Coll said bitterly.

"No, no, son! 'Lost' meaning no one knows where they are! No dead bodies found, nor no living ones neither!"

"Fled?" Coll looked up, a light of hope in his eye.

"I don't doubt it," Gar said. "Remember my concern about the soldiers who might have taken cover in the greenwood? Banhael will find many new recruits for his band, I think, but not very many women."

"Oh, there will be those, too," Mama said darkly. "Ours wasn't the only village trampled beneath the soldiers' feet, sir, I assure you! Already these vagabonds have heard of four other clusters of serf huts gone, and the people fled."

"There must be hiding places other than the forest," Gar said, frowning.

"To be sure, there are, and many of the men will find their way back to their homes, if their villages still stand. Many more will find their way back to their lord's castle, since they've no place else to go."

"But the bones of many others will someday be found, in the thickets and the crannies where they crawled away to die," Coll said, scowling.

"I fear so," Mama sighed. "Thus has it always been— thus will it always be, and we women must bring more men into the world so that humankind doesn't kill itself off completely."

"Perhaps it deserves to!"

"No, Coll, it doesn't," Gar said gently. "Who began this war, anyway?"

"Who begins them all?" Coll retorted. "The lords!"

Gar nodded. "So if you take away the lords, perhaps the wars will stop, at least for a while."

Dicea and Mama stared in fright at the enormity of the treason Gar spoke, but Coll only laughed a short and bitter laugh. "That's what you've preached to Banhael, isn't it? But no matter what you said, he heard nothing about killing off the lords completely—he only heard a chance to become a lord himself! That's the only change that will come about if you slay them all, sir knight—new ones will arise, and worse than the ones before! They'd have to be, or they wouldn't have been able to kill the old ones!"

Dirk shook his head. "It's possible to keep the lords out, Coll. The people can band together and pull down any man who tries to boss them."

Coll stared at him, then recovered. "Band together? How? Under a leader! And what's to keep that leader from becoming a lord, hey?"

"The people," Gar told him, "if they're all armed and all trained to fight, and if there's a law that says the leaders can't do anything without their consent."

Coll stared at him as though he were insane. "A law? The leaders *make* the laws!"

"Doesn't have to be." Dirk shook his head. "The people can gather together to agree on what laws they want to make, then pull down any leader who tries to break those laws."

"A law stronger than a lord?" Coll stared at him. "Are you crazed?"

"No, Coll, and neither is Sir Gar." Dicea laid her hand on her brother's forearm, but her glowing gaze was all for Dirk. "If they say it can be done, it can."

Coll glanced at her face, saw more fascination with men than with laws, and knew there was no point in speaking any further. "Have it as you will," he said bitterly.

"It's worth a try," Mama said slowly. "Give them that much, son—it's worth a try. In fact, if the men leave it up to the women to decide, there will never be *any* wars."

Well, Coll had seen women come to blows, though not as often as men, so he found room to doubt. Even so, he had to admit the women would declare fewer wars than the men.

Gar nodded slowly. "I've heard of such an arrangement before—a men's council and a women's, with both needing to agree before any action can be taken."

"Why not simply have women in the same council?" Dicea seemed very excited by the idea, so excited she couldn't keep it in, but she spoke very softly, as though trying not to be heard.

Gar nodded gravely, though, turning to her. "That has been tried, too." He shrugged. "Each people seems to have its own needs and requires its own form of council."

Coll stared. "Do you mean to say that every people is governed by a council?"

"A system of councils, I should say," Gar said slowly, "and I have heard that some peoples are better governed without any such meetings—but I have never seen any."

"Do you mean to tell me that the outlaws are ruled by a council, not by Banhael?"

"The outlaws *are* a council," Dirk explained. "They're a small enough group so that everyone can speak up—and they did. Banhael was constantly talking with one man, three men, five, persuading, intimidating, asking—but he couldn't just command, except in battle. They didn't have to meet as a council—they met for dinner every night—but they were a council anyway."

Coll stared at him; then his eyes lost focus as he remembered what he had seen of the way Banhael spent his day. Dirk was right—he had been constantly chivying and haranguing. "Will these mountebanks prove to be a council, too?"

Dirk shrugged. "We'll have to see. Whatever else they are, they should be great cover for five people on the run."

"Cover?" Dicea frowned. "How do they cover us?"

"A hiding place, Dicea," Gar explained. "If we disguise ourselves as vagabonds and travel with them, no one will think to look for us among them."

Dicea stared. "Knights disguise themselves as vagabonds?"

"Is it any worse than hiding among outlaws?" Dirk countered.

"I've disguised myself as worse, to escape when my side has lost," Gar assured her.

"But the king won!" Coll exclaimed.

"Yes, but many of the Earl's troops, and some of his knights, escaped and are roaming the countryside," Gar told him. "We'll have to move carefully in seeking to rejoin the king—very carefully, and very slowly."

Coll lifted his head, understanding. Gar didn't want to rejoin the king—at least, not right away. Why? Well, that didn't really matter. All that did was that Gar and Dirk were bound on wandering for a while. And if they wandered in the company of that red-haired wonder, Coll certainly had no objection.

"The mountebanks should be glad of an armed escort, then," Gar observed. "If we hide our shields, no one will know we're knights unless they've already met us."

Dirk nodded. "After all, we don't wear any more armor than your average heavy trooper."

Dicea's eyes were wide; she looked scandalized, but was trying (unsuccessfully) not to let it show. Coll only grinned and nodded; it was the kind of ruse in which he was beginning to delight. "Shall I hide my spear?"

"No, we'll claim we're mercenaries, and we hired you to do the dirty work." Dirk grinned. "No lie like the truth, eh? Just hide your royal tabard."

Coll pulled the tabard over his head and folded it. "Done."

But Mama looked worried. "What if a king's knight discovers you?"

"Then we tell him that we're traveling in disguise to learn more about the lords and their weak points," Dirk told her.

Again, Coll thought, no lie like the truth.

"One could almost wish our side had lost," Gar sighed. "Then there would be no fear of someone accusing us of being deserters."

"Not much worry about that, anyway," Dirk pointed out. "After all, we left in such a hurry that we didn't get paid."

It didn't seem to bother him much at all.

The greybeard still seemed nervous when they rode out to join his carts as they came rumbling along the road, but he also seemed reassured not to see any armor, and only swords and daggers at the knights' hips, so he forced a smile. "Well met, sir knights! I am Androv. We are proud to have you join us."

"Well met, Master Androv." Gar inclined his head politely. "I am Sir Gar Pike . . . this is Sir Dirk Dulaine . . . Coll . . . Dicea . . . and their mother, whom I believe you have already met."

Androv smiled at Mama, and his nervousness fell away. "Yes, and an excellent companion she is, too."

And an even more excellent cook, Coll thought. He knew Mama was the only reason the mountebanks were willing to travel with the knights at all—not that they had much choice.

Mama smiled warmly. "How good of you to say so, Androv!"

"For the time being," Gar said, "I think we would do best to drop our titles. I am simply 'Gar' to you, and my companion is 'Dirk.' "

"You don't want people to know that you're knights, then?" Androv asked in surprise, then quickly shook his head. "No, of course, that's no business of mine! Come along, sirs, and since there are more woods ahead of us that are infested with bandits, we'll be very glad of the company of three armed men." He glanced at Coll. "You are armed, aren't you?"

Coll grinned and pointed to the first cart. "While you were talking, I hid it in there."

Androv looked in surprise and saw the butt of the spear poking out from the side nearest them. He smiled slowly. "Your hand was quicker than my eye, Coll. Have you thought of taking up conjuring tricks?"

Gar and Dirk laughed, but Coll perked up. "Why not? I can use all the training I can get!"

"What professor wouldn't give his chair for an attitude like that!" Gar sighed, earning looks of puzzlement from everybody.

"Why would a professor be so far from a university?" Androv asked—which put him ahead of Coll, who didn't even know what a professor was.

"To find students like Coll," Dirk replied.

Androv shrugged off the cryptic comment and got down to business. "You should know your companions by name." He turned to gesture toward his fellow mountebanks, beginning with those who were perched precariously on the carts. "Constantine . . . Charles . . . Frederick . . . Ciare . . ."

Ciare nodded courteously enough toward Gar's rough-hewn countenance, but her gaze lingered on Coll's face, becoming slumberous. He felt as though he were a field with seeds shooting out of the ground, and his smile seemed to glow in response to hers as he nodded.

Dicea frowned and asked, rather loudly, "Who is that handsome young man who drives the second cart, Master Androv?"

"Oh, that's Enrico," Androve said. The youth ducked his head, and came up with a long and caressing gaze for Dicea. She gave him a brittle smile in return—very brittle because Dirk didn't even seem to have noticed; he only nodded gravely to Enrico, then at each of the other players in turn.

Coll felt a little angry in defense of his sister, and could almost have felt sorry for her—"almost" because she had turned to chatter brightly to Gar. Coll turned an inquiring glance toward Mama, but she only shrugged and shook her head.

So they journeyed on, the men taking turns walking and riding in the carts, the two knights riding alongside and, from their higher vantage point, chatting with the players who were perched on top of the loads. Coll was amazed at how quickly they managed to draw out the players, at how easily the players were chatting, as though with old friends.

They came to a town about midday—a collection of wattle-and-daub huts with a few half-timbered buildings, two of which actually had a second story. There was a church, too, built of stone and a little taller than any other building, with a steeple besides. Androv went around it, off to the second largest building.

Coll looked about him wide-eyed, and so did Mama and Dicea. "I have never seen so many houses!" Dicea breathed.

Ciare laughed, looking down at her from her seat on the cart. "You'll see towns like this often enough, and many times bigger, too, if you stay with us long."

Dicea's face set in resentment at the reminder that she was a country bumpkin, but just then they passed the market, and her eyes widened again at the sight of so many booths, roofed with gaily colored cloth. She started toward them, but Mama caught her arm and pulled her back into line. "Later, darling—and after we've earned a few coppers, if we can."

They went around the largest building, and Coll was surprised to see that it was hollow. They came in through plank gates between two tall wings into a wide courtyard. Cattle lowed in a pen against one wall, pigs in a pen against another. Chickens pecked for grain in the dust, around the wheels of several carts held in place by wheel chocks; the horses and donkeys were stabled under a thatched roof at the far side of the courtyard. Hostlers moved about among the animals, and a kitchen was sending forth odors of roast pork and fresh bread that made Coll's mouth water.

A large man with an apron tied around his middle came up to them, his smile of greeting fading as he looked them over—but he kept his tone polite. "Good afternoon, travelers. What would you like?"

"A place to perform, landlord." Androv doffed his cap with a flourish. "Have I the pleasure of addressing the proprietor of this establishment?"

"You have." The landlord's interest kindled as he looked over the smiling players and the gaily painted canvas folded over the wooden trunks in the first cart. "Are you play-actors?"

"That we are, sir, and with many a fine play to present! We have the doleful history of Pyramus and Thisbe for lovers, the battles of Henry the Fifth for those of martial spirits, and the confusions of the Imaginary Invalid for those who love to laugh! Will it please you to have us perform them in your yard?"

Dirk muttered to Gar, "Interesting to see what survived from the original colonists." Gar nodded, and Coll wondered what they were talking about.

"That it will, that it will!" The landlord nodded and held out a hand. "I am Eotin. How much would you charge to let folk into the yard to see the play?"

"Only a shilling, sir."

"That's usual." The landlord nodded judiciously. "We share it shilling for shilling?"

"Of every two, one for you and one for me," Androv clarified, "with two meals a day, and rooms while we stay."

Eotin shook his head. "Rooms only for the leading players. The rest can sleep under the carts, as they do on the road."

"Well, if it must be, it must," Androv sighed, overdoing it. "Shall we perform this afternoon, landlord?"

Eotin looked startled. "Can you, so soon?"

Androv grinned, and several of the players laughed. "Give us bread and ale and a few hours' time, and we shall have your play fitted. Where shall we set up our stage?"

"There, of course, opposite the gate." The landlord pointed. "A few hours is scarcely time enough to spread the word and rent the courtyard rooms at the higher rate, but it should send rumor buzzing through the town to work harder than bees. Yes, by all means, a short play this afternoon!"

"We shall set to it," Androv promised. "If you could send the bread and ale of which you spoke . . ."

"Yes, of course!" Eotin nodded and turned toward the kitchens.

Androv turned back to the drivers. "Bartholomew! Chester! Back the carts up where he showed you!"

A hostler appeared by Dirk's stirrup. "Shall I stable your horse, player?"

"Huh? Oh, sure!" Dirk dismounted, yanked his saddlebags off, and let the hostler lead his horse away while he turned to help Mama down. Coll helped Dicea, to her annoyance, and stableboys led the ponies off. The two carts backed up tailgate to tailgate next to the inn wall. Androv held up a hand with a shout as the two bumped together. Other players set wedges under the wheels and drove them in tight with hammers, then climbed up and began to unload the carts, swinging the trunks down to other players on the ground. In minutes, the two carts were empty. Then the players on the carts pulled the sides, front, and tailgates out of the holes in the floor that held them and handed them down to the men on the ground, who passed timbers back up. The men on top fitted the timbers into the holes that had held the sides, fitted crosspieces between them, and started hanging curtains.

"Have you ever heard of trade unions?" Dirk asked Gar.

"Heard of them, yes," Gar answered.

"These guys haven't."

Coll wondered what a union was. He had only heard the priest use the term, and then only when he spoke of marriage—"holy union." Could Dirk and Gar mean these players were bonded in a sort of marriage? And if they were, could it be holy by any stretch of the imagination?

The players were hanging a second curtain in front of the first now. When they were done, one of them pulled on a rope, and the curtains parted. Coll stared in surprise, and Dicea clapped her hands in delight. "How clever!"

The player with the rope pulled it a second time; the curtains closed, and he nodded in satisfaction. "Our stage is set. How is the tiring house?"

"Done and ready," Victor called from below.

Dicea frowned. "What is a tiring house?"

"The place where the players change costumes," Androv told them. "Would you like to see it?"

"Oh, yes!" Dicea exclaimed, and Androv led them behind the carts. Victor was just finishing fitting a run of steps into the front of one of the carts; the one on the other side was already in place, and Alma stood at the top, hanging curtains on a set of pegs that stuck out from the top of a timber. Victor stepped aside, and Elaine climbed up to take the far side of the curtain and begin to hang it.

"The players will climb up and down the steps to make their entrances and exits," Androv told them, "and pass through slits in the curtains at the bottom." He led them inside, and they found themselves in a space about twelve feet by eight. Against each wall, a crossbar hung from the uprights with pegs along its length. Elspeth and Drue were hanging up costumes.

Dicea looked about her wide-eyed, but Mama clucked her tongue in disapproval. "Anyone in a room above can look down and see the women as they disrobe!"

"They wouldn't see much," Drue told her with a laugh. "We never wear less than our shifts during a performance. We only change robes on the outside."

Victor laughed, too, as he set aside his spade and reached up to catch a long, five-inch-thick pole Constantine was handing down to him. He set its base into the hole he had been digging. "We'll hang a roof from this, good woman, and make a proper pavilion of the whole thing. Don't worry—not even a bird will be able to see in from above."

"It would spoil the illusion if they saw us changing," Androv explained.

"What lovely dresses!" Eyes shining, Dicea reached out to touch a velvet gown.

"Ah, please don't, lass." Androv reached out to intercept her hand. "That belongs to Catharine herself, not to the company."

Catharine looked up at the sound of her name. She was middle-aged, like Mama. "Are your hands clean, lass?"

Dicea glanced at her hands, then nodded. "They are, Mistress."

"Then go ahead and touch it. It *is* lovely cloth, isn't it? That was given me by a duchess's maid, for her mistress had just cast it away, and the maid could not wear such rich stuffs, of course."

"But actresses can?" Dicea asked, eyes wide.

"Yes, but only when we're playing a part."

"Then I must be an actress!" Dicea exclaimed.

The players laughed, and she looked around wide-eyed and reddening—but Androv only nodded gravely. "I've heard of worse reasons for wanting to tread the boards of a stage. But there's a great deal of hard work in it, lass—and a great deal of learning to do, if you really want it."

"I do!" Dicea cried. "And I've a lifetime of hard work before me no matter what I do!"

"But you may not have the gift of mimicry," Androv cautioned her.

"And you may tire of fending off the attentions of noblemen and their gentry," Duse told her with a dark glance at Magda, who glared back. "Some of them take actresses for strumpets, you know."

Dicea shrugged angrily. "The lords and knights will take us for their strumpets no matter what we do."

"Dicea!" Mama gasped.

"Why not say it, Mama?" Dicea said scornfully. "It's only by Coll's fighting for me that I escaped, the one time that I was too late feigning dowdiness and dullness."

Ciare turned, staring. "You can make yourself appear to be so unattractive that the knights pass you by?"

"Doesn't every serf girl learn the trick of it?" Dicea asked.

"No—most only try." Claire turned to Androv. "Perhaps she does have the gift, after all."

Dicea stared, then smiled in delight. She whirled to Gar. "And what part will you play, sir knight?"

"What part, indeed?" Duse gave him a sleepy, inviting look.

Gar smiled, amused. "Defender of Innocence."

They all laughed, but Androv only smiled, nodding shrewdly. "That might do, young sir, that just might do. Not of innocence, perhaps, but a defender? Oh, yes, you might do that quite well—if you were willing."

Gar turned to him, still smiling. "Just what did you have in mind, Master Androv?"

9

The performance began early in the afternoon. The landlord, Eotin, had sent his stableboys to the market to spread the word, and the audience started filing in as the sun neared the zenith. Androv's youngest players—boys, really—stood at the gates to collect pennies from everyone who entered. One or two men tried to push past the boys without paying, but each time, Gar stepped out in front of the man, rumbling, "I think you forgot to pay the boy, goodman."

"Wha . . . ? Oh, yes! So I have!" And the gate-crasher turned back to pay his score, grumbling under his breath.

Androv stood by, nodding in admiration. "Well done, my friend, very well done indeed. Usually one of us stands by to back up the boys, but you're far more effective."

Gar shrugged. "Sometimes ugliness has its advantages."

"You, ugly?" Androv glanced up at him keenly. "Some of our young women think otherwise. I'd take it as a favor if you ignored their charms, friend Gar."

"To do otherwise would surely be no act of friendship." Gar smiled. "I assure you that, unlike the law, I *am* a respecter of persons."

When the innyard was full, Androv slipped around behind the back of the crowd with the boys and Gar, to the tiring house.

There, turmoil met them. "Master Androv!" Elspeth cried, "Jonathan is ill!"

"Ill indeed." Mama stepped up, nodding. "His forehead is hot, and he's racked with stomach pains. Something bad in his food, I doubt not."

"Will he be all right?" Androv asked in alarm.

"I think so, but we'll have to keep watch over him. And it will be at least three days before he's well, perhaps a whole week."

"Well, that's a relief." The chief player relaxed, then suddenly stiffened again. "Who will play the knight?"

"Why, Axel can," Elspeth said.

"The armor won't fit him! It won't fit anyone but Jonathan!" Master Androv tugged his beard in frustration. "Let me think! What can we do?"

"Do you really need the knight?" Gar asked.

"Of course we need the knight! Who else will lead the villagers against the giant?"

"That much, Axel *can* do," Gar said.

"How ridiculous! A mere peasant, lead others against a monster? No one would ever believe it! The audience would boo us off the stage!"

"On the contrary, it's *completely* believable," Gar told him. "Try it. At the worst, the audience will be so surprised they won't say anything at all."

"It would be new, it would be alive!" Axel's eyes glittered with anticipation. "Let me try it, Master Androv!"

"We haven't much choice, have we?" Androv sighed. "Very well, lads—Axel shall lead the peasants against the giant. Now quickly, into costume and onto the stage, before the crowd tears us apart with impatience!"

A few minutes later, the boys, resplendent in tarnished tabards that had once graced a duke's heralds, stepped out on the stage with trumpet and drum to beat a quick tattoo accompanied by a loud, if somewhat off-key, fanfare. The crowd quieted a bit, and Androv stepped out on the stage to begin the prologue. "Hearken, good people! Attend and see! The tale of Gargantua on our stage shall be!"

A murmur of anticipation ran through the audience. Coll was in an excellent place to hear it, for it was his task to work his way through the crowd, keeping a sharp eye for rotten fruit and overly enthusiastic admirers of actresses, not to mention those overly fond of ale. Unfortunately, there was plenty of fruit and ale both, for the landlord's serving maids were twisting their way among the spectators selling their wares—from one glance at a fruit tray, Coll could see Eotin was taking advantage of the opportunity to get rid of some of his outdated merchandise.

But it was so difficult for Coll to keep his eyes on the people about him when Ciare and Duse were stepping so lightly about the stage in their finery, discussing the horrible giant who was nearing their village. Their movements were graceful, their gowns low-cut, so Coll was hard-put to restrict himself to quick glances at the pretty actresses and spend most of his time watching the customers. Still, he managed it, seeing Androv come out to try to shoo the girls away, for the giant was coming. They shooed, but as soon as Androv had hurried away, they came back, giggling at the fun of lying in wait to see the giant.

Then he came, Gargantua himself, and the whole audience gasped with fright at the sight. So did Coll, stunned by the enormous size, the bulging naked muscles, and the horrifying mask. Then he remembered that "Gargantua" was only his master Gar, and relaxed—mostly; at the back of his mind was the nagging realization of something he had forgotten, that Gar really was that huge, that formidable.

Well, not *quite* that huge. He wore three-inch soles on' his boots, and the mask rose up a foot above the top of his head, making him look far taller than he really was.

He shambled over to Ciare and reached out, caressing her hair. She stood trembling a moment, then screamed and ran—or tried to; Gargantua caught her arm, and she twisted against his pull, falling to the floor. Duse dropped to her knees, hands to her cheeks, and cried, "She's dead! You horrible monster, you've killed her!" and ran screaming from the stage. Alone, Gar knelt, almost breaking his ankle in those thick-soled shoes, and reached out to touch Ciare's hair again, then lifted her head, lifted her arm . . . Coll realized the giant was trying to make the girl dance with him again. When he realized he couldn't, his shoulders sagged, and his whole body seemed one united expression of unutterable sorrow. The audience quieted, amazed at the monster's tenderness, and heard one muffled sob.

Then Gargantua rose, fumbled in a pouch at his side, and brought out a mouse. Several women gave little screams, and several men gave exclamations of disgust, before they realized it was only a puppet. The little creature frisked to and fro on Gargantua's palm, and he reached out a finger to pet it gently. His huge frame straightened; his whole body seemed to lighten, to cheer up. Restored, he put the mouse back in his pouch and stumped off the stage again.

Thus the story went—Gargantua always trying to be friendly, always seeking to touch in affection, but always destroying, never understanding his own strength. After each encounter, he sought solace by playing with the mouse again, even after three men banded together and came at him with flails. But at last he petted the mouse too hard, and it broke. Then Gargantua let out a howl of unutterable grief, sank to his knees—and rose with anger and hatred. It was then that Axel shouted to the other peasants, harangued them, telling them they must save themselves, and led a charge against Gargantua with swords, scythes, whatever weapons came to hand.

The giant turned to strike out against the pack. He

hurled them from him, one after another, until they all leaped upon him together, flailing and stabbing. The audience went wild, cheering and booing—some for the peasants, some for Gargantua. At last, the mound of churning bodies stilled, and the men rose to carry the inert body of the giant off the stage.

Androv came back on, to thank the audience for their attention and admonish them to give the stranger the benefit of the doubt, then ending with a plea for applause. They gave him more than he asked for, and the company filed out to bow, Gar still in mask and buskins. Then, as the applause died, Androv called out, "Tomorrow, an hour after noon, the tale of the Imaginary Invalid! Good evening, friends!" He waved as the players left the stage, then followed them.

The applause ended, and the spectators filed out of the innyard, chatting with excitement about tomorrow's play. Coll elbowed his way through them, hurrying to get back to the tiring house and see whether or not Gar had collapsed from the strain.

He hadn't; he was grinning, the mask in his hands, as his fellow players heaped praise and acclaim on him.

"You were excellent, Sir Gar!" Duse stepped up right against him, eyes shining. "I have never seen so moving a giant!"

Gar laughed with pleasure. "Yes, but if you had seen my face, I'll warrant you wouldn't have been half so impressed!"

"Oh, I'm sure we would have!" Elspeth crowded in, also right up against him. "Your every movement, your every grunt and growl spoke oceans of emotions!"

"Why, thank you!" Gar inclined his head, but kept the mask in his hands. "If I had been given a word to speak, though, I'm sure I would have shamed us all!"

"Well, you didn't!" Dicea crowded in, too, closer than

she ever would have dared if she hadn't seen the actresses do it. "You were noble, overwhelming!"

"Really, most excellently done!" Androv stepped up, shooing the girls away, and clapped Gar on the shoulder. "It was a stroke of genius to have Axel lead the peasants! Did you hear how that audience cheered them? How did you know they would?"

"Why, I didn't *know*, of course," Gar replied, "but I've learned that no one likes to see anything so much as himself—if that self is disguised a bit."

Androv nodded slowly, interest kindling in his eye. "Are you sure you've never acted before?"

"Not on a stage, no." Gar was still grinning. "And I beg you, don't make me do it again—at least not in any part that has lines."

"Give the man a stoup of ale!" Androv cried, and steered him toward his clothing. "Come, pull on your garments, and let us tell you of the next work we have in mind for you. No, not on the stage, don't worry; the Imaginary Invalid has no part for a giant."

"I should think not!" Gar laughed, and the two of them were off to chat as Gar pulled his clothes back on.

Disappointed, Dicea stepped over to Dirk, batting her eyelashes. "Shall you be a player, too, sir?"

Coll wondered when his sister was going to make up her mind—and whether or not it would do her any good.

"Only in the right game," Dirk said, grinning, "and for the right stakes."

"Oh? And what stakes are those, sir?" she said with a saucy smile, stepping a little closer.

Dirk abruptly sobered. "Peace, and the end of all these wars the noblemen wage. Freedom would be a nice added fillip, but I'll settle for one thing at a time."

Dicea stared, taken aback by the enormity of it. Then

she recovered, gave him a look of mock exasperation, and said, "You can become so stuffy so easily, Sir Dirk!"

"Indeed," Ciare said, stepping up to Coll's side. "Can *you* be playful, sir, even though your master is not?"

Dicea flashed her a look of annoyance, but Coll favored her with a long look and an intent smile. Her eyes met his directly, and he felt as though some force was speeding from her into himself, making his whole body thrum like a fiddle string. "What game did you have in mind?"

"Ducks and drakes," Ciare answered, just as Dicea said, "Roundelays," and they were off into a three-way contest that featured hidden meanings and not-so-subtle innuendos. Coll found himself wondering whether he was really a player—or only a referee.

The next day, Elspeth and Duse vied for the honor of showing Gar his duties when he wasn't acting; diplomatically, he stated that he needed both points of view and strolled about the innyard with one on each arm. Ciare stayed out of that competition, only guiding Coll to show him his duties. Of course, Gar really didn't need a half-hour's tour and explanation of how to hold the horses of the gentry while they watched the play, and Coll certainly didn't need anywhere near an hour's coaching on how to roll a rock across a sheet of iron to mimic the sound of thunder. Coll did have to admit that he was asking for far more detailed explanations than he needed to, but he noticed that Dicea kept dropping in on Dirk from time to time with one unnecessary question after another, so he felt justified.

At last Ciare led him through the curtains behind the two carts into a large tent with the stage as one wall and the inn for another, with canvas above them and canvas to each side. "This is the tiring house," she said.

"How does one tire?" Coll asked.

Ciare turned to him, smiling, leaning back against the inn wall. "Why, one tires by long exercise."

"Then I must have tired you in this long excursion, especially with all the questions I have asked." Coll's heart beat faster; he hoped the beckoning in her face was really there, not only the result of his wishful thinking. He stepped closer, and her smile widened, eyelids half closing.

"Not so much effort by half," she said, her voice low and husky. "Can you not give my mouth more exercise than that?"

Coll stepped closer still, his face mere inches from hers, their bodies almost touching, and smiling into her eyes, feeling his whole body tingling with her nearness.

"You are too distant," she breathed.

He kissed her, then kissed her again, longer—then again and again, longer and deeper each time.

From that time on, Coll and Ciare were always careful to be very decorously well apart from one another—but they found frequent opportunities to be alone.

Coll had to admire the skill of the older actor-women with their needles—but his sister's skill was another matter. She was soon sitting beside Dirk every chance she could make, asking him all sorts of questions, finally hitting on the matter of government and war, and settling herself to listen to a lecture. Unfortunately, her smile faltered a few times, and her boredom began to show.

But there wasn't enough time for Dirk to become too elaborate in his subject. As soon as the bread and cheese had been washed down with ale, the players were up and rehearsing. They breezed through the show so quickly that Coll found himself wondering how they could make it last long enough for the audience to feel they'd had their money's worth. Dirk seemed to think so, too, for he asked Ciare, "Only an hour?"

"No, they're just practicing the difficult parts," she told him, and gave Coll a look that said she would enjoy practicing herself. "With the audience, it will last several hours."

"Several hours of pleasure would be well worth the effort," Coll murmured, gazing into her eyes. Then he gave himself a shake and asked, "How does the innkeeper make enough money from this to be so eager to have you perform? Do you pay him?"

She nodded. "One penny in two—but most of his money he makes from the knights and lords who rent the rooms that look out into the courtyard—the only time he can charge more for them than for those on the outside." She gestured at the second-story rooms and the porch that ran in front of them. "He charges for the food and wine they eat, too, of course."

"Sounds like a wonderful way to spend the afternoon," Coll said, with a look that made the statement ambiguous.

"I would love to have the chance, someday," she returned, fluttering her eyelashes.

"Even if the play were boring?"

"Our play would be anything but tiresome," she assured him. "Even if it were, though, a knight and woman could simply retire into the room and draw the curtains."

"How could you lose?" Coll leaned a little closer to her.

"They come! They come!" Androv bustled up to them. "The apprentices lead them! The audience nears our gates! To your stations, one and all!"

In a few minutes, they were trooping in, the young bloods handing their horses' reins to Gar and one or two of the younger players where they sat by the hitching rail. When anyone tried to push past the boys taking coins, Gar rose from his seat, towering over the gateway, and the customers suddenly remembered where they had put their money.

Soon the patrons had formed a long line, jostling elbows and chatting merrily as they waited—merriment that grew as the landlord's potboys passed up and down the line with wineskins, pouring flagons for anyone who paid a penny. One or two chafed at the delay, though, grumbling about the unfairness of it. Coll, holding horses, could scarcely believe his ears when he heard Gar say, "Be glad you're only waiting for a play to begin, friend, not waiting for the next battle to start.''

People fell silent around them, staring, appalled. The grumbler turned on Gar. ''Oh, we're always waiting for that! But at least we don't have to stand idle, or pay to be admitted!''

''Of course you pay,'' Gar said, ''in blood and ruin. What you really need is a playscript for war, so that only the evil are slain.''

Startled silence greeted the statement, a silence that erupted into shouts of laughter. Even the grumblers had to grin. ''Well said, play-actor! But where will you find such a script, eh?''

''In the courage of common folk,'' Gar answered. ''Did you see the play last night?''

''With the giant Gargantua? Aye! A brave tale, that!''

''Brave indeed,'' Gar agreed. ''Where was the knight or the lord when the giant came?''

The people fell silent again, staring. Some began to glance around them nervously.

''Why, that's right.'' It wasn't the grumblers who spoke, but a merchant with grey at his temples. ''There wasn't a knight, was there?''

''The play called for it, but the actor who played him was sick,'' Gar said. ''Did you miss him?''

The merchant's eyes kindled. ''Not a bit!''

''Nor did I,'' one of the grumblers said, frowning.

Coll wasn't sure he wanted to hear any more.

''That's the way plays are,'' Gar told them. ''When you see knights and lords, you have wars.''

''Only in plays?'' an apprentice asked. He was beginning to look angry.

But the line moved forward then, and Gar was saved from an answer. Instead, he turned with interest to the next knot of grumblers, who were complaining about not being able to see very well. ''The lords can,'' Gar told them.

Coll gave the reins he was holding to a stableboy, and went inside to see how Dirk was faring. He hoped nothing would happen to Gar, but the giant's words were raising both his anger and his hope. He told himself the day's work would be enough.

He found Dirk quickly—and wished he hadn't. He was telling a handful of journeymen and apprentices, "There are only three people in each cell. That's right, people— women can be just as good at passing information as men. But each person knows someone in another cell, and each of *them* knows another."

"So no one knows more than four people?" a journeyman asked.

Dirk nodded. "The three in his own cell, and one from another."

"So if word needs to travel, only one cell needs to be told." An apprentice lit up with enthusiasm. "Each of its three tells one from another cell, so four cells know! Then each of the three new cells tells others, and thirteen cells know!"

"And on and on, so that within a day or so, everyone knows." Dirk nodded. "That way, the ones who are planning the action can make sure . . ."

Coll hurried away before he could find out what "the action" was. He was already shaking with fervor, and he had to last through a long afternoon. Could Gar and Dirk really mean it? Really mean to haul down the lords, and stop the wars? Or at least to curb the noblemen, to impose some sort of law on them, too?

"Audiences are usually far more unruly than this."

"Uh?" Coll looked up, and found that his steps had taken him to Androv. The chief player swept a gesture out to include the whole audience. "I've never seen people who only laugh and talk and throw the occasional apple core! Usually there are loud quarrels, fights breaking out, women squealing as men make improper advances." He shook his head, marveling. "Your masters have an amazing way of calming a crowd, friend Coll."

"Amazing indeed." But Coll wasn't all that sure that their way was calming. For the time being, maybe, but he had a notion they would prove quite exciting in the long run.

When the performance was done, Gar and Dirk lounged about, not near enough to overhear much that went on between Androv and the innkeeper as they counted the money, but very obvious and in sight of Eotin, in case he decided to change the terms of the agreement. Coll stood near them, quivering with frustration. Now, when he could ask the dozen questions they'd stirred up in him, now when he could swear to do anything they asked if only there were a real chance of muzzling and chaining Earl Insol—*now* the knights only wanted to talk about the performance, and the players!

"They have enthusiasm," Dirk pointed out.

"Oh yes, tremendous enthusiasm!" Gar agreed. "Of course, their delivery is, shall we say, grandiose, and their concept of characterization comes straight from the carpenter's shop—but they do it with zest!"

Dirk shrugged. "They have to make their voices heard all the way to the far wall, and their gestures have to be clear to people a hundred feet away and two stories up. Of *course* they're going to be big!"

"And subtleties of character . . . ?" Gar prompted.

"Won't be clear beyond the first row. Of course, it might help if they stuck to the script . . ."

Gar's shoulders shook with a silent laugh. "It might help if they *had* a script."

"Of course." Dirk smiled. "But since they don't, and since their only reason for performing is to make a few pennies, you have to rate them according to whether or not they put on a good show, not their achievement as artists."

"Which, of course, they would probably deny being,"

Gar sighed. "Was it really from such rough and ready beginnings as these that Olivier and Evans and Omburt grew?"

"You forgot Shakespeare and Molière."

"No, *they* did. You can see how it must have been—the scripts were lost, the serfs were forbidden to learn to read, but the actors passed down the plays from father to son and mother to daughter by word of mouth. They forgot the lines, but they remembered the story itself—so their descendants go out on the stage and make up the lines as they go along."

"But why did the original colonists let some serfs be players?" Dirk wondered.

Gar shrugged. "What else are you going to do in the evening?"

Coll could think of a few answers to that, any of which would have made more sense than what the two knights were talking about. Apparently Dirk could think of them too, because he gave Gar a slow smile, but only said, "I can see your point. A play would be a welcome change now and then, wouldn't it?"

"Very much," Gar agreed, "but *only* as a pastime. These bush aristocrats aren't the kind who care very much about art, after all."

"They do have a few rough edges," Dirk admitted.

"And would have rather drastic ways of treating players who failed to amuse, I doubt not," Gar said grimly. "No, all in all, I would have to admit that what these players do, they do well."

"Exactly." Dirk nodded. "We just shouldn't be expecting them do to anything more—or trying to. After all, they probably don't even know it exists."

"But they stay alive," Gar agreed, "and free of serfdom, though I suspect nobody raises the issue."

"Come, woman! You cannot pretend to any great store of virtue!"

All three men turned to look, suddenly alert for trouble.

Four men had gathered around Ciare, chatting and laughing, and though the oldest had made the comment with a joking tone, his face was quite serious.

"I think they might want some more company there." Dirk nodded toward the group, and Coll said, "Yes," as he strode, hands balled into fists, feeling anger hot within him.

"Let me know if you need reinforcements," Gar called, then leaned back against a post, arms folded, watching with interest.

"Pish, sir!" Ciare gave the man a playful push away. "Do you think that just because I walk onto a stage, I'm bereft of purity? For shame!"

"Shame?" Another man chuckled. "Everyone knows that player women don't know what the word means." He reached out toward her bodice.

Ciare gave his hand a playful slap. "We know it quite well, as knights seem not to! The king wears jewels in his crown—do you think that because you can see them, you should touch them?" She took a step back, right up against the chest of a tall young man, who reached around a groping hand, chuckling. "It's not the king's jewels that we speak of, lass, but your own charms." His arm tightened about her, and Ciare tried to pull it loose with a cry of distress. The men laughed.

Coll couldn't take it any longer. He forgot the law said that a serf must not raise his hand against a lord; he forgot about the noose; he could only think of Ciare being forced to the pleasures of the lordlings. He reached out to seize the nobleman.

10

━━━ formatting ornament ━━━

Ciare saw him reaching, and cried, "Coll, no!"
But another hand intercepted Coll's, holding him off in an iron grasp, and it was Dirk's other hand that caught the lordling's wrist and squeezed. The young blood cursed and twisted his hand free of Dirk's—and of Ciare's waist, but he was too busy glaring at Dirk to notice. "Who are you, fellow?"

"A gentleman who had a prior claim on this young woman's time." Dirk stepped up to him, nose to nose, though he had to tilt his head back to do it. "Do you dispute that claim?"

The young blood glanced down at Dirk's hand on his rapier's hilt and grinned wolfishly. "Why, here's a poxy bold fellow! Do you know to whom you speak?"

"What does it matter?" Dirk retorted. "Corpses need no names."

The young blood's grin hardened. "But they have them, and their kin take unkindly to those who slew them."

Dirk shrugged. "So you have a large number of corpses, all with the same name. Is that an improvement?"

The young blood snarled and pushed Dirk away, leaping

back himself to draw his rapier. Dirk's steel flickered out to guard only a second behind. The other young bucks started to move in, but someone nearby cleared his throat very loudly. All four of the playboys looked up—and suddenly became less willing to play, because it was Gar who stood nearby, hand on the hilt of a sword longer than any of theirs, towering over them all by almost two feet and a hundred pounds of muscle. He was only watching the proceedings with interest, but the backup group took the hint and backed off.

"The landlord won't like spilled blood in his innyard," Gar said. "Be quick about it, will you?"

"We'll see whose blood is spilled!" the young gentleman snapped, but with more volume than emotion. He leaped forward, thrusting.

Dirk parried, then whirled his sword in a figure eight as the young blood advanced. He thrust, and Dirk's sword rang down, striking the rapier so hard it spun away into the dirt. Its owner cried out, shaking his hand in pain. While he was distracted, Dirk stepped up and twisted the dagger out of his left hand. The young blood stared at him, suddenly realizing how completely he was at Dirk's mercy. His face went white.

Dirk sheathed his sword and took the injured hand. "Here, let me see." The young blood tried to pull away, then shouted more with alarm than pain as Dirk's left hand closed tight on his forearm. Dirk's right probed the other's sword hand gently. The man winced and ground his teeth. Dirk dropped the hand and stepped back. "Nothing broken—but I didn't think there was. Probably a sprain, though. You should wind a bandage tightly around it and let it rest for a day. Some brandy would help—inside you. Not too much, though."

The young blood blinked, surprised that his late opponent should care.

"Here, take him home," Dirk said to the backup group,

then turned to Ciare, who was watching from the safe haven of Coll's arm. "Androv says you have work to do setting up for tomorrow's show."

"Yes! Of course. Thank you." Ciare gave him a glance of gratitude, then went past him toward the stage, Coll following.

Dirk watched them go, saying to Gar, "That fast enough for you?"

"Yes, quite," Gar answered. "Lacking a bit in finesse, mind you, but certainly effective."

Dirk shrugged. "You didn't say to make it pretty."

Coll was inside the tiring house only a minute, then came out to see Dirk and Gar coming toward him, while behind them, the young gentry were escorting their friend out of the innyard with awed glances back over their shoulders. Coll knew just how they felt. He stepped aside for Dirk and Gar, deciding they were his masters indeed.

They came through the tiring-house curtains and found Ciare standing, hands on hips, looking about her. "I thought you said Androv wanted me here!"

"He didn't," Dirk said.

"I do," Coll told her.

She darted into his arms, head on his chest. "Oh, you darling fool, I was so afraid you would strike that lordling and have a dozen soldiers fall on you!" She looked up at Dirk. "Thank you, thank you, Master Dirk, for saving him for me!"

"Anything to oblige a lady," Dirk said gallantly, "which you are, by your behavior if not by your birth."

Ciare gave him a dazzling smile, which became slow and languorous as she turned back to Coll.

"I believe it was *you* that Master Androv wanted," Gar told Dirk.

The smaller man replied, "Did he? Guess I don't hear so well these days. Well, let's not keep him waiting." He led Gar out of the tiring house without a backward glance.

"My employers are understanding," Coll said to break the sudden silence.

"Understanding what you meant by saying that you want me, you mean?" Ciare turned her head a little away, regarding him through her lashes. "Well, then, you have me. What do you wish to do with me?"

For answer, Coll lowered his head and kissed her. He meant it to be short and respectful, but Ciare's hand pressed down on the back of his neck, and the tip of her tongue danced over his lips, galvanizing him, so the kiss became far longer than he had intended. When it was done, he had to cling to her for a few minutes before his head stopped swimming.

Ciare laughed softly and pushed herself a little away from him. "What else do you wish to do with me?"

"Many things." For a moment, Coll's mind spun with possibilities—but they frankly frightened him, so he answered her smile with one of his own. "But not necessarily here. Those young swaggerers have left the innyard now, so there's no need to stay hidden. Let's step inside. I think the rest of the company is sitting down to supper, at the landlord's expense."

"Will you take me in on your arm?" Ciare demanded.

For answer, Coll proffered his arm. She slipped her hand inside his elbow and went with him, laughing.

Coll sat beside her throughout dinner, and noticed that Ciare never said a word about the young men who had accosted her, or Dirk's way of dealing with them, but she was even more attentive to Coll than usual. Dicea gazed at them, fuming, for a while, then turned her attentions to Gar. He chatted with her gravely and with courtesy, managing to work her into the conversation with three of the other actresses who had made a point of sitting near him. As the servers were bringing out the pudding, Coll realized that it had been some time since Gar himself had spoken more than a few words; somehow he had managed to coax all four women into a discussion about the frustrations and pains of dealing with men. Gar still listened impassively, but Coll had to turn away, his ears burning, and listen somewhere else.

The next morning, Gar asked Androv, "Do the young men in the audience always pester the actresses?"

"Always," Androv confirmed, "though Magda and Drue don't seem to think of it as pestering, if the young bucks are handsome enough. For the others, though, we must be watchful. They've become expert at discouraging young men gently, but some refuse to be discouraged, and have to be diverted by other means."

So after that day's performance, Coll made sure he was by Ciare's side right after the ending, and Dirk was right beside him, so the young bloods were clustering around a trio, not a woman alone. Nonetheless, a young knight swaggered up to elbow Coll, crying, "One side, fellow! Don't keep the sugarplums all to yourself!"

"The actress's time is taken," Coll told him.

"Oh, is it indeed!" Today's young blood dropped a hand to his sword hilt. "And what if I should like to take some of it?"

But Coll stood like a boulder, and Dirk turned to face the young buck, hand on his own hilt—but two others sidled up to Ciare. "Oh!" she gasped, as a hand touched her bottom, and "Sir!" more angrily, as the other man touched her breast.

Dirk swung about, eyes flashing, sword half-drawn, and steel whickered as the man behind him drew, too.

"No!" Ciare cried in distress. "Please, no! I will—"

"You won't!" Coll shouted.

"Let go!" the young blood behind him raged.

Everyone turned to look, Dirk with only a quick glimpse that showed the swaggerer with his sword half drawn, frozen by a huge hand which had closed on his, holding the sword where it was.

"Gently, gently, now, sir!" Gar soothed. "What kind of gentleman would force his attentions on a woman who didn't want them?"

"Want them! Of course she wants them! Why else would she parade her charms before the public that way?"

"Why would the men who play parts on the stage 'parade'?" Gar countered. "Or do you think they do it to attract women to buy their favors?"

"Well, of course not! For a man, it's different!"

"But this woman, and all her friends, have only the same reason as the men," Gar explained, quite reasonably, "to present a story for your entertainment, and the money they gain is only that which comes at the gate."

The man glared up at him. "Do you mean to tell me none of these women sell their favors?"

"I've never seen them do so." Gar didn't mention that he had been with the troupe only a few days. "Better to ask yourself how many women of the common people *do* go willingly to the bed of a man not their husband."

"Why . . . they seem willing enough when I ask them."

"Willing?" Gar said skeptically. "Or scared to refuse?"

The man straightened, throwing his shoulders back. "Look at me, fellow! What woman would *not* wish to bed me?"

"Any who wasn't in love with you," Gar returned straightaway, "and if you deceive yourself into thinking that they choose to go with a total stranger out of sheer desire, you deceive yourself indeed. Any woman who makes so free with her body does so out of fear or hunger, or both."

The young blood glared in indignation. "Do you say that I am not a fine figure of a man? And with a handsome face, too!"

"I wouldn't know," Gar said. "I'm not a woman. But I do know that no matter how attractive a man is, a woman must be wooed for a few days—or weeks, or months— before she desires to share his bed."

The young man frowned, peering more closely. "You don't sound like a man common-born. What are you?"

Gar gave him a sardonic smile and, in a tone that gave the lie to his words, said, "Come, now. Would a lord, or even a knight, travel with a band of players?" He stared directly into the young man's eyes.

The young man returned the gaze, holding it level as he said, "No," and, "Of course not."

Coll heard the words, but also the tone, and knew that Gar had confirmed the young nobleman's guess, and the young nobleman had accepted the knowledge as a secret that would be kept.

There was a new tone of respect in the young man's voice as he said, "I am Dandre, heir to the Earl of Mauplasir. And you, sir?"

"Gar," the giant told him, "just Gar. How do you think of your serfs, my lord—as people to be protected, or worldly goods for your own pleasure and amusement?"

"People to be protected, of course!" Lord Dandre said in indignation. "Certainly they must do their work, but it is the lord's obligation to protect and care for them!"

Gar nodded. "And serfs who are not your own?"

"Why, you treat them with the respect you would show to any other kind of property belonging to another lord . . ." His gaze strayed to Ciare, who clung to Coll, watching with apprehension. "Do you say that I have broken my own code?"

"You have, though I suspect you had no idea you were doing so. You assumed that because the lass was a player, she would be eager for any lord's attention—but if she had been a serf on your own estates, you would not have assumed so."

"Not the one following the other as summer follows spring, no," Lord Dandre said slowly, "though there are surely serf girls aplenty to vie for a lord's favors. Still, I have never pursued one who did not make it clear that she wanted me to do so." His face firmed; he turned to Ciare, sweeping off his hat in a bow. "Your pardon, lass. I mistook."

"Certainly, my lord," Ciare answered, wide-eyed. "I thank you." She glanced at Gar as though to wonder what wizardry he had performed. So did the young man's companions, though they, too, had begun to look rather thoughtful.

"You are knights," Gar pointed out. "What did you swear to do when you were knighted?"

Lord Dandre frowned. "Why, to protect the Church and to fight for the Right, but there's never much need for that."

"And to defend the weak?"

"Yes, and the honor of ladies, especially . . ." Dandre's voice ran down as he glanced again at Ciare. "But she is a woman, not a lady!"

"Is it only the wellborn, then, that you're supposed to defend?"

Lord Dandre looked at Ciare in consternation, and his friends began to mutter darkly to one another.

"Perhaps you think that women of the common people can protect themselves," Gar said, "but think—you're also supposed to protect the poor, and the weaker from the stronger. What is a commoner woman but just such a weaker? And these players, I assure you, may be numbered among the poor."

The backup group quieted, frowning at Gar.

"You mean, then, that I should certainly defend all women," Lord Dandre said quietly, "not ladies only."

Gar nodded. "If not because they're ladies, then because they're poor."

"And that I should defend the weaker, herself, against the stronger—*my*self." Lord Dandre's smile was tight with self-contempt.

"You have named it, my lord. Oh, I have seen soldiers

bring a virgin kicking and screaming to their lord, for no better reason than that she was a serf, and pretty. To do them justice, young men of our—*your*—class are taught that all serf women are eager to leap into bed with them, if only for the money which will be sent them if they prove by child. But that is simply and plainly not true; it is a fable handed down from father to son, when neither ever asked the women themselves."

"Why, then, how could we know the truth?" the young man exclaimed with anger. "But if it is as you say, then my misguided notions nearly led me into virtual rape!"

"There is no 'virtual' about it," Gar said severely. "No means no, my lord, no matter of what class the woman may be. Even if 'no' means only that the woman isn't sure she's ready to say 'yes,' even if it means she is wanting to say yes and is *almost* willing to, it is still no."

" 'Willing' isn't enough; the woman must be eager, or I am exploiting one weaker than myself." Lord Dandre's face was red with anger. "A pox upon the vile rumors that have ever led me to believe otherwise! I thank you, friend, for showing me this! I shall tell this truth to all who speak of it!"

"This isn't the only untruth about their serfs that noblemen believe," Gar assured him. "How many of the lords you know have serfs who are well housed and well fed, my lord?'

"Why, well enough, for serfs," Lord Dandre said, surprised.

"Are they truly, my lord?"

Lord Dandre frowned again. "You must think otherwise, to ask me with such weight. Nay, friend, rest assured that from this day forth, I shall look more closely at the poor folk around me!"

"Thank you, my lord," Gar said with a little bow. "I think you will be surprised at what you see."

"Surprised or not, I shall thank you ever more! And if I

find the poor folk to be as miserable as you say, I shall ex-
hort all young lords to work to defend them!"

Gar looked down at the ground, pressing fingers over
his lips, then looked up with a forced smile. "I am delighted
to hear you speak so, my lord—but may I caution you not to
be too outspoken on the issue? Indeed, I would enjoin you
to be very careful to whom you speak about it."

Dandre frowned. "Surely it cannot be so dangerous!"

"But it is. Think, my lord—by saying that lords are
obliged to lessen the sufferings of the poor, you're limiting
the power of each lord to do as he pleases within his own
demesne—and there are some lords who will not take
kindly to any such limits, no matter who imposes them."

Lord Dandre stood gazing into his face for a minute or
more, then abruptly nodded. "A wise caution. Again I
thank you." Then he turned to Ciare, doffing his hat. "Lass,
again I ask your pardon!" Then he turned to his friends,
clapping his hat back on his head. "Come! Let us go study
the poor folk, and see how deep is the truth this stranger
has told us!"

They went on out the innyard gate, walking fast, and Gar
turned to Ciare, who was sobbing on Coll's shoulder. She
looked up at Dirk and Gar through her tears. "Thank you,
my protectors! I could not have borne it if it had happened
again!"

"Again?" Coll went rigid, but managed to hold back the
questions and only hold her, resting his cheek upon her
hair, waiting for the sobs to pass—and slowly, the tension
bled out of him.

When Ciare's sobs slackened, she turned a tear-streaked
face to Gar and said, "I cannot thank you enough, Sir Gar,
for having saved us from spilled blood."

"I'm not sure I would have minded doing a little spill-
ing," Coll grated.

"Oh, I know, my brave one!" Ciare pressed a hand

against his chest, looking up into his eyes. "I was so frightened that you might strike to defend me, and be spitted on the young nobleman's sword!"

Coll stiffened, but forced a smile and touched her cheek gently. "I don't think *I* would have been the one struck down."

"Even worse! For then they would have fallen upon you in a pack and beaten you senseless! And when you waked and found yourself in irons, they would have tortured you before they hanged you! Oh, I could not have borne losing you! Please, oh please, my brave one," she implored him, "vent your anger on me if you wish, not on a man whose only real fault was that he was misguided! You heard what he said to your friend, even now! He didn't know!"

Coll drew a sharp breath. "What a generous spirit you have, to be able to forgive so easily!"

"But rightly," Gar said. "The young lord does have some sense of noblesse oblige, after all; he only needed his obligations made clear to him."

"And you did so with great skill and gentleness!" Ciare turned back to Gar. "Oh, thank you, thank you, for holding them away with words, not with blows!"

"It was my pleasure," Gar said gravely, "but it imposes an obligation on you, lass, one which I'm sure you have already fulfilled—to never say 'no' if you don't mean it, or at least aren't yet sure you mean 'yes.' "

She stared at him, breathing, "I never have!"

"Nor did I think you had, as I have said," Gar assured her, "but there are many women who aren't willing to accept that responsibility. Of course, they will never really be women grown then, will they?"

Ciare frowned. "I don't understand what you mean."

"That's all right," Dirk said. "Neither does he."

"Lord Dandre is really a good young man, but misguided," Gar told them. "If he tells what he has learned to other young lords, we may see the wars ended out of sheer duty." He turned to Coll. "Is there a chance of it?"

Coll's smile was sour. "I'd like to believe it, Master Gar, but there have been young lords of good heart before, many times before."

Gar frowned. "What happened to them?"

"Their fathers died," Coll said simply, "and they became lords in their own right. Then they changed, as I have told you." He shrugged. "A lord is a lord, Master Gar. Maybe it's the coronets they wear that infect their brains."

"Perhaps," Gar said darkly, "or perhaps it's the power."

Coll shrugged again. "Coronet or power, what can be done about it?"

"Leave them the coronets," Gar told him, "but take away the power."

Coll stared, feeling fear chill him at the mere thought. What kind of man was this, who could speak so easily of curbing the lords?

They performed once more the next afternoon, but the innyard wasn't quite so fully packed as it had been the day before, and the innkeeper told Androv several of his courtyard rooms had gone unrented. Androv knew the signs, so he thanked the man and told his players to pack. They took down the stage, filled the carts, spent one more luxurious night sleeping in real beds and had one more breakfast cooked in a kitchen, then rolled out of the innyard and onto the high road when the sun was scarcely above the horizon. As they passed the outskirts of the town, Kostya and Chester veered away from the carts and went jogging off the road through a screen of bushes. Coll was very curious, but he knew better than to ask.

Half an hour later, Coll was getting worried. "Look," he

told Ciare, "we'd better tell Androv that two of his players are missing."

"He knows," Ciare assured him.

"Yes, you all know each other's business, don't you?" Dicea said acidly.

"Always," Ciare said, amused. "We're like a big family, in a way."

"And I've noticed how well the brothers and sisters get along," Dicea said darkly.

Ciare laughed outright. "Or fail to, you mean? Yes, we have our rivalries—and yes again, we're very much like two children vying for their parents' favor."

"Or two sisters vying for the same suitor," Gar said. Both women gave him a glare, but he only asked, "You know the song, don't you?"

That took them by surprise, and both stared at him. "Which song?"

"The song of the two sisters," Gar said, and sang them the tale of the woman who pushed her younger sister into a river so that she might win the younger's lover for herself. They listened enthralled; Gar gave them the nicer version, in which the miller tried to save the girl and buried her when she died, but her breastbone rose to the surface, and a minstrel made a harp of it—a harp which, when he played it in her father's hall, sang the story of the elder sister's treachery for all to hear.

As Gar was finishing, two figures darted from a grove just ahead of them—Kostya and Chester, each with a fat chicken under one arm, the other holding the beak shut. They leaped up, and friendly hands hauled them aboard the carts, where they burrowed under the cloth and among the trunks to disappear.

Coll stared, scandalized, and Dirk asked, "Just what have you two been up to?"

"It's a crime to let a stray chicken wander off to become

the prey of a fox," answered a voice from the interior of the cart.

"The fox should know," Gar said, amused. "Are you certain those chickens were strays?"

"Quite certain," the other voice assured him. "We made sure of it ourselves."

"You just couldn't stand to see them penned up and fretting to have a nice walk outside their coop, eh?"

"Who should know better than those who love the freedom of the open road?" Kostya's voice countered.

"Then let us hope you continue to enjoy that freedom, boys," Androv said, and shook the reins. "Gee-up, you! Go a little faster, there!"

11

―――ᴡɯʍꜰꜱꜰᴡɯʍ――

T he Duke of Trangray erupted when he heard the
news. "That arrogant child! That overweening prince-
ling! How dare he assault one of his elders!"

The spy who had brought the news knew better than to
try to answer. Trembling, he crouched, hoping it would pass
as a bow, and backed toward the door half a step at a time.

"How dare you bring such atrocious tidings!" The Duke
stepped up and backhanded the man across the face. He
flew toward the wall, but one of the guards put out a hand
and caught him. "Pay the man and send him back to learn
more!" the duke snarled, and his seneschal nodded and
took the spy aside.

"Bad enough for him to attack, but worse for him to
win!" Trangray fumed, pacing the room. "His grandfather
tried it when he first came to the throne. Every monarch
tries it when first he rises! The crown seems to infect them
with this ridiculous notion that simply because they wear
jeweled gold on their heads, they have the right to command the rest of us! But my father beat his grandfather
home and left him to rule only his own estates all his life,
and I shall whip his son in similar fashion!"

"You shall indeed, Your Grace," the castellan agreed. "However, this proud stripling now has most of Earl Insol's soldiers to drive before his own."

"What matter? I shall have more! There's not a one of us ten dukes who doesn't know how vital it is to teach a new monarch his place! Send heralds to each of the other nine, Sir Lochran, and tell them the news, then tell them that Trangray says we must band together to teach this strutting peacock chick a lesson straightaway, or he will take it into his head to try to conquer us one by one!"

The players were all asleep, and the campfire burned low, almost as low as Gar's and Dirk's voices—but Coll was still able to hear them, and the nonsense they were talking was troubling enough to keep him awake. Still he tried to sleep—he kept his eyes closed and strove to relax, to ignore their words—but found he couldn't.

"Traveling with these players is an excellent way of setting up an underground," Gar said, "but how are we going to keep the separate cells in touch with one another?"

"It's a puzzler," Dirk agreed. "It's one thing in a city, where the different cells are so close together that no one has any problem arranging a way to bump into his contact—or even in a forest, where there isn't going to be too much worry about secret police watching when Banhael sends a messenger to each of the smaller bands. But how do you bring it off when there're twenty miles of open country between villages, and lords' soldiers all over the place?"

"We could have Herkimer run up a hundred transceivers," Gar suggested.

"Isn't that getting a little obvious?" Dirk asked. "The lords are bound to notice a cultural intrusion of that magnitude."

Gar nodded. "More importantly, so will the Dominion

Police, if they happen to have an agent touring the planet at the moment.''

"You can never tell with those guys," Dirk sighed. "They might be there or they might not. Give 'em their due—their disguises are foolproof.''

"And we're no fools.''

"Just lucky they weren't around when you stirred up our little revolution on Melange.''

"It was scarcely 'little,' " Gar said stiffly, "and the Dominion Police couldn't have done anything about it even if they had discovered it—it was all being engineered by people who'd been born on the planet!''

"Except for a certain very tall party who just happened to be the focus of the whole thing.''

Gar shrugged. "Even then, I was just assuming a role your dead genius had prepared for me five hundred years earlier—and I was just the trigger.''

"True," Dirk said judiciously, "and since the lords already had radio transceivers and all sorts of high-tech gadgets, there wasn't really any worry about upsetting the cultural applecart.''

"Here, though, it could be a very different matter," Gar pointed out.

"Yeah." Dirk made a wry face. "They don't even remember what an electron is!''

Gar nodded. "If we taught them to use radios, some of the bright ones would start wondering how they worked, and within a generation, they'd have begun to suspect the answer.''

"And in three, they'd have electrical power stations, radios, three-dimensional television, and microwave networks, all grafted onto a medieval culture . . .''

". . . And the monarchy would become a hereditary totalitarian dictatorship," Gar pointed out, "with a vastness of oppression which would dwarf the slavery we're trying to curb now!''

"Maybe not." A new light gleamed in Dirk's eye. "If they don't remember any technology higher than a hammer, anything we do bring in, they'll dub magic. What's the matter with that, in a medieval culture?"

"A point," Gar sighed, "and if technological magic can work, we might just as well call in the Wizard."

"Of course!" Dirk slapped the side of his head. "I keep forgetting there's more to you than there seems! Yeah, call him in!"

More to him than there seemed? Coll looked up and down the giant's frame. If there were more to Gar than that, it must be mighty indeed!

"Let me think it over, while we contact more malcontents and outlaw bands." Gar rose to his feet. "It's not one of those things that I do lightly, Dirk."

"Yes, I've come to realize that." Dirk rose, too. "It is a bit of a strain on you, isn't it?"

"There is that," Gar admitted, "but I can bear it. What really bothers me is that it always seems to be taking unfair advantage."

"Unfair advantage?" Dirk stared at him. "You've got knights in full plate armor massacring unarmed civilians and sending their soldiers out to burn down villages, and you worry about unfair advantages?"

"Yes, that's why I've resorted to it a few times," Gar sighed, "and probably will again. But this time I had hoped not to."

"How else are two guys from out of town going to turn over the whole social-stratification heap?" Dirk demanded.

"There probably is no way," Gar admitted. "Still, it bespeaks a lack of skill. I can't rid myself of the notion that I ought to be able to do it all by strategy."

"Oh, fine! You scheme, while more serf-soldiers get wiped out in another skirmish between dukes! And you had the gall to talk about noblesse oblige!"

"True," Gar said, looking as though he had just bitten into a bad nut. "Let me sleep on it, Dirk."

"Good idea." Dirk turned toward his blanket roll. "I could do with a few winks, too. After all, we need to contact more outlaw bands before we do anything."

"Yes, and many more malconents," Gar agreed. "I do have a little time, don't I?"

So they went to bed, but Coll lay awake another hour or more, excitement thrilling through his blood. Not only were they actually trying to throttle the lords—they really had done it before! He had no idea where Melange was, but if they said they had brought about this "revolution," this turning of the wheel there, told it to each other when they thought no one else was listening, why, then, surely they had! And they had magic for the doing of it! A wizard to call upon! Was he the "Herkimer" they kept mentioning? And would they really call upon him to work this miracle?

Coll didn't pray often, but he prayed that night—and, by praying, finally managed to fall asleep.

"Away with you, fellow!" The guard pulled back his hand to slap the bent old beggar, but the man straightened up suddenly, and his eyes flashed with anger. He spoke with the air of authority, the unquestioned assumption that he would be obeyed. "Tell the duke I am come."

The guard hesitated, hand still pulled back; the man's very voice, his accent, bespoke him to be of the gentry at least. On the other hand, he could be an impostor. The guard studied the face before him carefully, and stiffened, seeing a hint of someone he knew under the thatch of white hair and beard. "Who . . . who shall I say is here?"

"That is not for you to know, villein! Send word to your master, and conduct me to his audience chamber!"

The guard had always lived by the rule of passing any

problem out of the ordinary on to his officer. He capitulated and led the beggar in to the captain of the guard.

The Duke of Trangray was infuriated by the virtual summons, but the captain of the guard seemed so certain of the importance of the old beggar that the duke came to the audience chamber. "What is your wish?" he demanded.

The old beggar turned to face the duke, stepping forward so the guard and the captain were behind him, then pulled the false beard from his face. The duke stared for a full minute. Then he turned to the captain and said, "Leave us."

The captain knew better than to argue or ask. He ushered his guardsman out and left the two alone.

"So the rumors that you were captured were false!" Duke Trangray exclaimed.

"As you see, my lord duke." Earl Insol bowed. "But I shall not soon forget the humiliation that our puppy of a king has forced upon me in order for me to escape. May I ask your hospitality?"

"Given, and gladly! Come, we will see you equipped as befits your station!" The duke led his guest through his private passage to his own chamber and gave him a robe, then summoned serfs to bring hot water. While the earl bathed, the duke sent garments of his own. An hour later, bathed, shaven, and dressed in rich robes again, the earl joined his host for the midday meal.

Before they could begin, a servant stepped in. "Your Grace, you had asked to be told the instant the messenger arrived."

"He had better have good news," the duke snapped. "Show him in."

The servant bowed and went out. The duke turned to Insol and said, "Four of my brave fellow dukes have sent word to say that the king's estates are far from their own, so they see no reason to march against him—but they encourage me to chastise him, and wish me well!''

"The craven scoundrels," Insol said with a curl of the lip. "If it were not for you, the king would gobble them up one by one!"

"Yes, and they are content to let me wear myself out in fighting him," Trangray replied, "whereupon they no doubt intend to swoop down upon me and take all I have! So I shall not battle the king alone. But if I do not have at least a few more lords to fight beside me, I may not fight at all!"

The servant led a messenger in, still dusty with travel. "My lord duke!" he said, bowing low.

"Out with it, man!" the duke snapped. "To whom were you sent, and what is his answer?"

"The Duke of Grenlach, my lord." The messenger held out a scroll tied with ribbon. "He was outraged to hear the news you sent, and bids me tell you by my own lips that he will ride posthaste with ten knights and a thousand men!"

"A beginning, a good beginning!" Trangray's eyes gleamed. "Go find food and refreshment!" The messenger bowed and left, and the duke snapped open Grenlach's letter. "Look, my lord earl, and read the beginning of the king's doom!"

By the end of the week, all the messengers had returned. Four more dukes had sent word of outrage and a pledge of aid. In fact, they told Trangray they would be on the march by the time he read their letters, and asked what action he intended.

"They have chosen you their leader, my lord duke," Earl Insol said as they watched the couriers ride away with the duke's directions to his fellow warlords.

"They have indeed!" Trangray's eyes gleamed with pride as he watched the horsemen gallop off. "Come, my lord! We must ready our own army to march, for I've told my fellow dukes to advance on your own estates! There will we meet, to begin the disciplining of this would-be tyrant! To Castle Insol!''

"I thank you, my lord." The earl bowed. "It seems I shall return home sooner than I thought."

The players toured from one town to another, and in each one, large or small, Gar and Dirk managed to fall into conversation with serfs and merchants and young noblemen about "cells" and the hard lot of the peasants and the wrongs done to them by their lords. Coll began to develop a bad case of nerves at the second town; if any lord's man heard them, the whole company was liable to be clapped into irons, or worse!

Somehow, though, the axe never fell; Dirk explained that they were on their way again before their rabble-rousing could alarm the authorities. But with each town they entered, Coll became more and more apprehensive, and as they left each set of gates behind, he breathed with greater and greater relief—until the next town brought even more fear.

He couldn't understand why Master Androv didn't kick the two knights out of his troupe—though admittedly, the thought of kicking Gar out of anywhere was enough to freeze the blood of any man. Still, Coll knew the giant was so courteous that he would have gone without any fuss, simply by being asked—so why didn't Master Androv ask? Could it be because *Gargantua* always brought in so much money, and assured them of packed innyards every day they played? Surely he, Dirk, and Gar made themselves useful, helping pack the carts and unpack, setting up the stage and taking it down, and even marching onto the stage with wooden swords and spears, playing soldiers or messengers. Coll even managed a few stammering lines himself: "Milady, the thane approaches," or "Help, help!" Certainly Androv must have known what Dirk and Gar were doing, the alarming things they were saying! Could he really have seen no harm in it?

He must have, because the greybeard became quieter and quieter the longer they stayed with the company—but he never asked them to go. Could it be because the young bloods left off harassing the actresses when Gar stepped up behind them? Or because Dirk had a way of strolling up to any group of townsfolk who were jibing at the players, rattling his sword and coughing in a way that seemed to calm the hecklers amazingly?

Surely it couldn't have been because Coll himself was scarcely ever far from Ciare, or because Dicea fumed and sizzled whenever any of the actresses took time to chat with Dirk or Gar, especially since she took it out by flirting outrageously with every male in the company. Some of the townsfolk tried propositioning her, but Coll came up beside her quickly, real spear in hand. She scolded him for it when they were alone, and the next time the young bloods started making insulting, insinuating remarks, it kept on until Gar stepped up. When they went away, Dicea took advantage of the chance to show Gar just how grateful she was; he accepted her profuse thanks gravely, made sure she was well, and went back to work on the stage, leaving her sizzling worse than before.

So on top of dreading the moment the soldiers fell upon them, Coll also had to worry about his sister finally exploding, ranting and raving at the actresses and at Dirk and Gar alike. Fortunately, Mama was so good a cook, and so skilled with her needle, and had become so fast a friend of everyone in the little troupe, that they all would have forgiven Dicea in an instant, just for Mama's sake. Coll began to realize that his mother had done it intentionally.

So it was no surprise when one of the peasants, listening to Gar and Dirk and growing redder and redder with righteous indignation, finally burst out, "You're speaking treason! Guards! Arrest them all!"

A dozen men in cloaks threw them open, revealing the livery of soldiers, and drew swords as they fell upon the players, driving them into a knot in the center of the innyard with shouts and curses.

Dirk started to draw his sword, but Gar set a hand upon his, holding the rapier in its scabbard. "No. Our punishment might be visited upon the others." Dirk froze, and contented himself with glaring at the spy, who showed all his teeth in a grin. "Herd them up! So, gaffer, you thought you could defy the earl, did you?"

"I have defied no one!" Androv protested. "I don't have any idea what you're talking about!"

"Talking about! I'm talking about the talking these two have been doing, about lords catering to the whims of their serfs and lowborn soldiers refusing to strike at slaves who disobey! Don't tell me you know nothing about this!"

"Nothing at all!" Androv protested. "You don't think I would have let them stay in my company if I had, do you?"

"We're very discreet," Gar told the spy. "In fact, you wouldn't have suspected us at all if you hadn't just happened to be wandering around town listening for subversion, would you?"

The spy reddened again. "But I did hear you, and came back today to arrest you! Secrets always come to light, don't you know that?" He waved to his men. "Come, take them all!"

The soldiers moved in around the players, and Ciare turned on Coll. "You traitor, you snake! We took you in, we took you to our bosoms, and all the while you were endangering us all by preaching sedition! How vile, how unspeakable! Do you think we're nothing but toys to play with, mere pawns in your game? How could you, Coll? How *could* you?"

Coll turned pale but didn't answer, only standing rigid.

"Oh, aye, hold your tongue! There's nothing you *can* say, is there? You have wronged us, and there's nothing more to be said about it! Now we're all going to suffer in the duke's dungeon, and all because you couldn't be honest with us! We may be hanged for your lies!"

"But it wasn't you!" Coll burst out. "None of you! We kept it secret from you all, you *couldn't* have known about it! How could I imagine they would arrest you all with us?"

"A singular lack of imagination, for a player." The spy watched Coll narrowly.

Coll rounded on the spy. "I'm not a player, damn it!"

"True," Gar put in. "None of us three are players."

"I'm a mercenary, a soldier!" Dirk told the man. "Did you see us do any acting? No! We carried spears onto the stage and off it, we held the gentlemen's horses, we told the hecklers to shut up—we earned our keep! But did you ever hear any of us three say more than four words at a time on that stage?"

"No, there's truth in that," the spy admitted, and turned to Ciare. "You have convinced me, lass. It was all their doing, and none of your own."

Ciare stared, then whipped about to glare at Coll again, turning pale.

"I never asked for more than justice," he told her. "You're innocent; you shouldn't share my punishment." His voice sank to a whisper. "You've done right."

Her lips parted in a soundless cry, her eyes filled, and she turned away. Mama reached out and took the girl in her arms, and Ciare burst into tears.

"How touching," the spy said, with full sarcasm, "but I'm afraid we can't stay to see it. Put your arms behind your backs! Sergeant! Tie their wrists! That one, too!" He stabbed a finger at Coll. "He's one of them. I've seen how he stays near the big one as much as he can!" He turned on Androv. "He's theirs, isn't he?"

Androv glanced at the rest of his company, weighed those he could save against those he could not, and croaked, "Yes."

"Off with you, villein!" The spy caught Coll's shoulder

and spun him away to a soldier, who held him fast while another lashed his wrists behind his back. "You can rot in the duke's prison until he's good and ready to let you hang! Be off!"

The spy reached up to give Gar a shove. The big man started meekly off, hands already reddening from the tightness of the bonds. Dirk and Coll stumbled after him, but the serf's heart was singing with the relief of a partial victory. Dicea and Mama had stayed with the players, and the spy seemed never to have guessed they were tied to Dirk and Gar! Silently, he blessed Androv, who hadn't said a word to betray them. At least his mother and sister would be safe.

12

━━⫘⫘⟋⦙⟍⫘⫘━━

The jailer hauled open a huge oaken slab, and the guards kicked them in. They fell, rolling, and the spy called after them, "Preach your sedition in there!" He burst into gloating laughter, cut short by the boom of the closing door.

Coll recoiled instinctively from the slimy chill beneath him, struggling to his knees, then his feet, gasping for breath. But breathing through his open mouth didn't help much. He had never dreamed of such a stench! The smell of human waste competed with the stink of unwashed bodies for primacy of pong. The very air seemed thick with it, but that was probably because the whole big room was lighted only by one small barred window, far up on the wall across from the door. Manlike shapes sat listlessly in the shadows; others milled about aimlessly in the gloom. A few of these last turned in their direction and came shambling toward them, hunched and menacing.

Coll swallowed heavily and stepped a little closer to Dirk, who was just managing to climb to his feet. "What do we do?"

"I don't know," the knight answered. "What do we do, Gar?"

"Just what the spy said," Gar answered. "Preach sedition."

"I don't think this is the most pious congregation in the world." Dirk's voice hardened with tension. "They don't have the look of the kind who like sermons."

"On the contrary." Gar had risen to his feet. "They look like just the kind who would cheer the sort of things I have to say. You there!" He stepped out to meet the biggest of the advancing prisoners. "You look like a smart chap!"

"Smart enough to teach you your place," the Neanderthal grunted. He was a head shorter than Gar, but much wider, seeming more like a door than a man—a prison door. "I'm the Gaffer, and in here, what I say goes!"

"Goes right out the window, from now on." Gar glanced up at the source of dim light. "Yes, you do have a window. Better send your claim to give orders through it, because *I'm* going to be running things here."

The gaffer didn't growl, didn't bellow—he just slammed a huge fist at Gar's midriff, doubling over and following it with blow after jackhammer blow, very hard and very, very fast. But Gar saw the first one coming—how, Coll didn't know, it had been so fast—and dropped both forearms to block the Gaffer's punches, then pulled one fist out. The Gaffer slammed in one last blow. Gar took it with a grunt, and the Gaffer leaped back, but Gar caught him on the ear with a quick right cross. The Gaffer's head snapped to the side, and Gar was on him, hitting him in belly, chin, then belly again. The Gaffer folded, but brought his arms up to block, then slammed a fist at Gar's face. The giant blocked and counterpunched; the Gaffer's head snapped back, and he staggered away, still holding his arms up. Gar followed closely, keeping the series of blows going until, fast as a striking snake, the Gaffer ducked under his punches, hammered at his midriff, then came up to crack a fist into Gar's jaw. Gar rolled with the punch, but the Gaffer leaped after him, swinging a haymaker that would have laid Gar out, but the giant stepped inside the swing, catching the Gaffer's wrist and tunic, then turning, sticking out a hip, and throwing the prison king to the ground.

He pulled up on the man's arm as he fell, so that he landed on his side. The Gaffer roared in anger and scrambled back to his feet—but Gar stepped in before he'd recovered his balance, knocked aside a futile punch, and slammed a fist into the man's gut. The Gaffer doubled over, but Gar straightened him up again with an uppercut. The Gaffer's eyes glazed; he teetered, then fell.

Gar turned to glare at the other prisoners, panting hard, bruises already beginning to darken on his face. He grinned, but his smile wasn't pleasant. "I said *I'm* running things now. Anyone else think I shouldn't?"

The prisoners muttered to one another in consternation.

"Well?" Gar snapped.

They turned back to him, faces going straight. "No, my lord," one said, and another agreed, "You're the Gaffer now."

Gar nodded slowly, the grin subsiding, then gave his fallen opponent a push with his toe. "If I'm the Gaffer, who's he?"

"Only Liam the Smith now, my lord," another prisoner said, poker-faced.

"No, he's my sergeant." Gar nodded at Dirk. *"He's* my lieutenant, and if any of you give him any lip, he'll take you down almost as fast as I could."

Dirk stepped up beside him, letting his grin grow.

"Anybody doubt it?" Gar's voice cracked like a whip.

"N-n-no, my lord," another man stammered, backing up.

Gar nodded slowly, then lashed out another question. "How did you know I was a lord?"

"Why . . . your manner of speech, your bearing, your whole manner!" the man stammered, and the other men nodded and muttered agreement.

"But you must know I'm not a *real* lord," Gar pressed, "or there wouldn't have been any nonsense about a challenge from your leader. You would have all leaped upon me and struck and struck until I moved no more."

The men exchanged startled glances. Apparently they hadn't thought of that.

"What, do you mean to say you wouldn't dare?" Gar scoffed.

"Uh, Gar . . ." Dirk sidled up to him. "Maybe we ought to leave well enough alone."

"But it isn't 'well enough,' " Gar insisted, and to the prisoners, "Stop and think. If you strike down a lord, who's going to punish you for it?"

"Why, the soldiers," said one of the men, as though not believing that someone could even ask about something so obvious.

"And what will the soldiers do?"

"Throw you into prison until they're ready to hang you!"

"But you're already *in* prison," Gar pointed out.

The prisoners all looked startled, then exchanged thoughtful glances. One or two turned to look Gar up and down. Coll could almost hear their thoughts.

So could Gar. "Of course, not very many lords are as big as I am, nor always with friends who are such expert fighters."

Now the appraising glanced turned to Dirk. Still grinning, he stepped forward—and suddenly whirled, catching one of the appraisers by the arm and shirtfront, then whirling on to throw him howling into a handful of others. They went down with enough shouting to fill the whole room. Dirk stepped back, eyes glinting with satisfaction, and watched them disentangle themselves, then rise again. When the noise quieted, he admitted, "Lords *do* know more about fighting than serfs."

Coll was glad they'd been giving him lessons.

"The question is," Gar told them, "what do you have left to lose?"

"Why, our lives!" said another of the men, as though he were talking to an idiot.

"Really! You expect to get out of here someday, then."

They stared at him, amazed; then the anger began to grow.

Gar nodded with satisfaction. "When you have nothing left to lose, why not strike back? All they can do is kill you!"

"Aye, and send us to Hell," one man said bitterly.

"Will you go to Hell for killing a lord who grinds his people under his foot, and uses them for his own cruel pleasures?" Gar countered. "Or will you go to Heaven for trying to save his serfs from their misery?"

Again, they all looked startled.

"You're hitting them with too many new ideas, too fast," Dirk said to him in an undertone. "You're going to lose them."

Gar nodded. "Then I'd better jump to the summary." He raised his voice again. "You can fight for your freedom, and the freedom of all your kin! If I'm your Gaffer now, that's my rule: that I'll teach you how to fight, and when!"

They stared, too dazed to argue.

The former Gaffer stirred and groaned.

Gar knelt by him, put an arm under his shoulders, and helped him sit up. "I know it hurts, but it'll go away in time. You there! Get him water!" He looked down at Liam the smith. "You hit hard, friend."

The man looked up, startled by the word, and the tone.

"You're no slouch yourself," he said slowly. "Know a few tricks, don't you?"

"Yes, and I'll teach them to you."

Liam's eyes narrowed. "Why? Then I could beat *you!*"

"No, you couldn't." Gar's grin wasn't nice. "I'd still know more. In fact, I could teach you fifty, and I'd still know more."

"Better believe him," Dirk said, in a tone that implied he himself had found out the hard way.

Liam stared up at Gar, then nodded. "I'll learn them, then." He broke off as another man thrust a dipperful of water at him. He drank it at a draft, then gave the bearer a long, measuring look before he handed the dipper back and turned to Gar again. "So you're the Gaffer now, eh?"

Gar stared at him for a moment, wooden-faced, and Coll realized he was surprised at the quickness of the Gaffer's intelligence. Then Gar said, "I am, and Dirk here is my lieutenant—but you're my sergeant."

The man gave a grudging nod, then asked Dirk, "Could you beat me?" His answer was a slow grin, but Gar said, "Even if he couldn't, I would. Be satisfied with sergeant, friend."

"Good advice," the man admitted. "I'm Liam."

"Well met, Liam." Gar clasped his hand, then pushed himself to his feet, dragging Liam along with him.

The new sergeant stood, grinning up at his new gaffer. "You'll do. What's your first order?"

"A question. Do you have any poles in here?"

"What, something to strike at the guards with? They'd never!"

Gar nodded as though he'd expected that. "Go form your men into two lines, then. Dirk, would you take Coll and start these men on their training?"

"Why, sure." Dirk beckoned to Coll and went to the double line that was forming in response to Liam's barks.

"That one there." Dirk pointed to a big bruiser a head taller than Coll. "Show him how to do a hip throw."

Coll looked the man up and down and quailed inside—the brute outweighed him by a good stone or two. But he couldn't shame himself in front of Dirk, so he strolled up to the grinning ape, then shot out hands, whirled, and laid the man on the floor just as Gar had done to Liam. The sergeant chuckled at the victim's yelp of surprise.

Dirk nodded. "Okay, back in line. Let's take that a little slower now. Face me, Coll." He began the movements in slow motion, describing what he was doing every step of the way.

Gar watched them, nodding approval now and then. While they practiced, he strolled around the huge cell, inspecting the conditions. When the men finished practice, cursing and sweating, he let them rest and drink a little water, then put them to work with broken crockery, shoveling the malodorous straw off into one corner, which he thenceforth dubbed the "privy," and sternly forbade the men to answer a call of nature in any other part of the room. Then he set them to work scrubbing the floor with rags. There was plenty of water, at least, fed by a pipe through the wall, probably from the moat. There was a huge heap of more or less fresh straw that Liam had been using for his private bed; Gar divided it up so that every man had at least enough to lay between himself and the cold stones of the floor when he slept. By the time the jailers shoved dinner through the flap in the door, the huge stone chamber seemed surprisingly neat, and almost clean.

Liam looked about, nodding as he chewed. "You've done wonders already . . . Gaffer." He said the word as though it had a bad taste, but he said it. "I hadn't thought it was possible."

"Thank you," Gar said. "At least we can practice without tripping on offal. When will they bring fresh straw?"

Liam shrugged. "When it pleases them. Maybe tomorrow, maybe next year."

"Then we'll have to be careful about throws. In fact, we had better avoid them as long as possible."

Liam blinked. "You didn't hesitate to throw me—or to have your man Coll throw Boam!"

"Yes, but we knew how to make sure you wouldn't land full force. All of you will learn that, but I'd rather not have broken bones while you're learning."

"What's a 'gaffer'?" Dirk asked Coll.

Coll jolted out of a daydream about Ciare—her glowing eyes, her tempting lips. "A gaffer?" he asked in surprise. "It's what you call an old man."

"A village elder, for example?"

Coll frowned. "*Any* old man."

"So it's short for 'grandfather,'" Dirk mused. "Nice to know your culture still respects the wisdom of age."

Coll stared, thrown yet again by an alien concept. "What people would not?" Then as an afterthought, "What is a 'culture?'"

"The ideas a group of people live by, and the way they express those ideas in their daily lives and the things they make," Dirk explained. "I can see a lot that's good in your culture, Coll."

"But some that's bad, too?" The serf frowned.

Dirk nodded. "Authoritarianism. Your commoners are so used to taking orders that it never occurs to them to think for themselves. What do the forest outlaws do when they're on their own? What do these prisoners do? Look for somebody to give them orders! It's not just Liam's fault that he became Gaffer—they wanted him to!"

"No, wait!" Boam frowned. "We don't *like* being bossed."

"You don't like it," Dirk agreed, "but you don't know how to live without it." And he launched into an explanation of social structure.

The prisoners listened, wide-eyed and fascinated. They interrupted with loud exclamations of denial now and then, but Dirk explained, and convinced them that what he had said was true.

When the last ray of light was gone, and they had sought their meager piles of straw, Gar said quietly, "You would have made a good professor."

"Why, thanks," Dirk said, surprised. "But I don't think any college would want to include this subject in the curriculum."

The next day, Gar started them off with calisthenics, then turned them over to Dirk, who gave them basic lessons in falling—but only from their knees; he was wary of the stone floor. After the first few shouts of pain and anger, he let them get back on their feet and showed them the basic guard position, then some elementary kicks and punches. When they were sweaty and panting, he called a halt and asked, "When do they serve breakfast in this dump?"

"It's right over there." Liam pointed to the water trough. "As to food, they'll feed us in the middle of the day, then again when the cooks throw out the garbage, if there is any."

"Yesterday's twilight meal, huh?" Dirk nodded grimly. "Well, exercise is supposed to hold down the appetite for a while. Take a break, guys, then report to Gar."

Gar gave them his standard lecture on the cell system, then led them through another drill in unarmed combat. Coll was astonished that the guards didn't stop them, but apparently they were used to shouting and scuffling in the big cell, and never thought to look. Either that, or they didn't care.

Dirk, though, saw a man sitting in the shadows, head bowed, staying in his own corner. He went over to talk to the prisoner. Curious, Coll drifted up beside him.

"You're missing all the fun," Dirk said.

"Nothing in life can be fun," the man growled. "Go away and let me die!"

."Die?" Dirk knelt down beside him. "They don't even allow sticks in here, let alone knives! How're you going to kill yourself?"

"Starvation," the man snapped. "There's no one here who will stop me—and they'll all help me, too, by keeping the food to themselves!"

"And when you finally get hungry enough that you can't help yourself, and try to fight for a bite, you'll be so weak they'll be able to swat you like a fly," Dirk said, with distaste. "Anybody else ever try this?"

The man shrugged. "Every month or so. It always works."

"I can believe it," Dirk said bitterly. "What's so bad about life, though?"

"The lords!" the man burst out. "They take our food, they take our women, they make us wear ourselves out digging in the dirt! Who would want to live?" Finally he looked up, glaring at Dirk with hot, hate-filled eyes. "And you're one of them!"

"Yes, but I'm fighting them," Dirk pointed out. "That's why they kicked me in here as a traitor. Look, though—if you really want to die, why waste your life?"

The man frowned. "What do you mean?"

"Why not take a lord with you?" Dirk asked. "Or at least a knight? With the skills we'll teach you, you might even take two or three before they kill you."

The man stared. "Do you really think so?"

"I've seen it done," Dirk said.

The man surged to his feet—and almost fell; he was already weak with hunger. Dirk caught him, and he hung on, panting, "Show me! It's better this way."

They had to feed him before he was strong enough to get in on the martial arts classes, of course, but he listened avidly to Gar's teachings—and gave Dirk an idea. He began to chat with the others one by one, ferreting out those who were so consumed with burning hatred, and had lost so much in life, as to be suicidal. He persuaded them not to care how they died as long as they could take a few knights with them, then taught them to sing, to juggle, and turn handsprings. "You'll wander the back roads from village to village," he told them, "and carry nonsense rhymes from cell to cell. They won't make sense to you, but the cells will understand the messages they hide. I'll send new songs by other minstrels, with messages hidden in them."

"But when will we kill lords!" one would-be entertainer hissed.

"When the egg hatches," Dirk said cryptically.

"I never thought of training minstrels," Gar admitted when Dirk told him, "or of sending encoded messages in ballads. Stroke of genius, Dirk."

"Well, thanks," Dirk said, pleased. "It will be slow communication, but better than nothing."

"Much better," Gar agreed. "In fact, I think we'll find that the ballads will travel faster than any one person. When it's time to rise, we can have Herkimer hop us from one location to another, releasing ballads—or even dropping them to minstrels."

All the prisoners listened avidly as Gar taught them oral codes. "If you meet a man who you think might be of another cell, say, 'John the miller grinds small, small.' That's the sign. Then if he says, 'The king's son of Heaven will pay for all,' you'll know he is one of us, and you can pass your message. But if he isn't . . ."

"He'll look at you like you're crazy," Liam interrupted.

Gar nodded. "Another sign is: 'The mills of the gods grind slowly,' and the countersign is, 'But they grind exceedingly small.' Now, let's say you want to tell another cell that there are thirteen cells already formed, but . . ."

"Are there really?" Boam asked, eyes huge.

"Sixteen." Dirk nodded toward Gar. "He doesn't bother keeping count—that's my job."

A respectful murmur passed through the prisoners, and they all straightened a little, gaining heart.

Gar went on. "But there's always the chance that a spy might happen by and overhear. You don't want him to understand, of course, so you say it in code, like this: 'Mother Goose is sitting on sixteen eggs.' "

"So each cell is an 'egg'?" Liam asked.

"Yes, and 'Mother Goose' is our uprising. If someone tells you, 'The eggs will hatch next Fiveday at fourteen hundred,' that will mean that all the cells will rise against whatever targets they've been assigned next Thursday—Sunday is 'Oneday,' and you count from there—and 'fourteen hundred' is two o'clock."

"Two hours past noon, yes!" Boam nodded eagerly. "So eight o'clock in the morning would be eight hundred, and noon would be twelve hundred."

Gar nodded, but a third prisoner asked, "Will that happen soon? The eggs hatching, I mean?"

"Not so soon as I would like," Gar told him, "but sooner than you think. Back to practice, now."

Late in the afternoon, the guards shoveled in a load of straw that was only slightly used, fresh out of the great hall. Gar set Coll to binding some of it into imitation quarterstaves, and he set to teaching the prisoners how to use them.

They stayed two weeks. Then Gar told Liam, "It's time to leave."

Liam snorted. "How are you going to do *that*?"

Very easily, as it turned out. Gar produced a heavy knife that he had hidden in the folds of his cloak. Liam stared. "How did you get *that* past the guards?"

"They were much more interested in my sword and dagger," Gar explained. "When it's dark, boost me up to that window."

Before dark, he and Dirk went quietly among the men,

giving them the names of their cells—there were tawny owls and banded owls, chimney swifts and barn swifts, gray squirrels and red squirrels, on and on through the animal kingdom. Coll wondered how Dirk could ever remember so many and be sure he had it right.

Then darkness fell, and five men stood against the wall with four men on their shoulders and Gar on top, picking at the mortar between the stones around the window. Liam was just beginning to growl about wasted effort when a shower of mortar silenced him. It took an hour and four changes of men, but at last Gar handed down the barred window, followed by blocks of stone two feet long and a foot thick. They came and came, six, twelve, eighteen. Then finally Gar climbed down, and the last pyramid of men groaned and rubbed their bruises.

Liam could only stare at the empty hole above him. "Who would ever have thought that mortar would have weakened so?"

"No one," Gar told him, "so no one ever checked it."

"You could have had us out of here the night you came in!"

"I could have," Gar agreed, "but you would all have been killed or caught again. Now there's a chance most of you will make it to freedom." He turned around, his voice stern. "When you get out, creep to the back of the castle and swim the moat. I've been watching the moon, and it's new—there won't be any moonlight tonight. Those who can swim will pull those who can't. When you reach the far side, sneak down the hill from bush to rock to bush. No noise, understand? Absolutely no noise! And no taking revenge on the lords or their soldiers—save that till the eggs hatch! When you're five miles away from here, go where your cell's been ordered to go—some to the greenwood, some to the towns, and your cell leader has been told the name. There, start new cells. If you're caught and go to another prison, start cells there! Everyone understand? ... Good. Time to go."

13

The escape went without a flaw; the plan was, after all, very simple. Even the most fearful of the prisoners wanted his freedom so desperately that he managed to hold his jaw tight against cries of fear as his friends hauled him over the moat and out onto dry land. If any sentry did look down and see silhouettes flitting from shadow to shadow down the slope of the motte, he must have dismissed them as of no consequence—he was watching for people trying to get into the castle, not for people slipping out. The fugitives gained the cover of the trees and began to move off, not stopping to say good-bye or to congratulate one another on their escape. They knew they had only begun, and were far from being clear.

Coll, Dirk, and Gar slipped past the King's Town through ditches and behind hedgerows on the surrounding farms. Then, out in the countryside, they walked down the broad, packed-earth thoroughfare—having been in the dungeon for only a fortnight, they were far better dressed than most of their fellow prisoners, so they dared take the chance. They stayed alert for the sound of hoofbeats, though, or the sight of moving shadows. They saw none, of course—no one else was abroad in the darkness of the night.

"You seem troubled, Coll," Gar said gently. "Isn't it good to be free again?"

"Very good!" Coll said. "But . . . doesn't it bother you, Master Gar, that you may have loosed murderers and thieves upon the world?"

"Not a bit," Gar assured him. "I've taken the time to talk with most of them, and Dirk has chatted with the ones I've missed. There were three killers in there, it's true, but the men they slew were trying to kill *them*, or to ravish their wives or daughters."

"Soldiers?" Coll could feel his blood growing hot again.

"Two. The rest? Well, yes, most of them are thieves. They stole a few loaves of bread or a joint of mutton to feed their families. Some lost their tempers and cursed a soldier or a knight, and were thrown into prison after they'd been beaten. A dozen were poachers—again, out of sheer hunger. No, I don't feel badly about loosing them on the world. The only people they're apt to hurt are lords, knights, and soldiers."

Coll's faith in his masters was restored.

"You'll have your chance to strike back yet," Dirk assured him. "Besides, remember: Ciare is out there somewhere."

The blood sang in Coll's veins at the mere thought, but in the next instant, a feeling of doom fell over him. "She thinks I betrayed her," he muttered. "She hates me now."

"What could you do but follow our orders?" Gar said gently. "We'll explain that to her. She'll understand."

Coll hoped he was right—though he doubted he would ever meet Ciare again. Just thinking of it made his gloom deepen further.

* * *

They washed both themselves and their clothes in a small river by the pale light just before dawn, then filled their stomachs with nuts and berries and lay down in a thicket to sleep until twilight. That was the pattern of their lives for the next week: they walked by night and slept by day in caves and thickets, one always awake and on watch. Twice they bumped into their former prison mates and traded news. The whole group had managed to stay in touch, single members traveling from one cell to another even in just these few days. Not a one of them had been caught; all were safely hidden. Some had taken shelter with robber bands. Coll wondered how long it would be before each band housed several cells.

Coll watched the sun and the moon, and realized their path was curving, heading back toward the royal demesne. Finally he asked Gar, "Are we going back to the king?"

Gar nodded. "We'll tell him we were split off from his army in the battle, and have been trying to make our way back to him without being caught. It's almost true."

"But it's been two months!"

"It could take that long, believe me," Gar assured him, and he had so much the air of a man who had done it before that Coll subsided, and didn't question him further.

Gar judged they were far enough from the duke's castle to risk being seen, so they began to travel by day and stop to exchange news in the villages they passed. He bought horses, too, so they traveled faster. After a few days, they began to come across the signs of soldiers passing—trampled crops, bruised peasants who told them they had no food to give or even to sell because the soldiers had taken it all, and here and there, a burned farmstead—so it was no great surprise when they came into a woodlot and heard screams ahead coupled with angry shouts, overlaid by gloating laughter.

Coll kicked his horse and charged ahead. Dirk caught

up to him, calling, "Make sure you're not fighting for the bad guys!"

"If there are soldiers," Coll called, "I'll know!"

Then they rounded the curve and saw the players' cart with one ox dead in the traces, and laughing soldiers carrying away Ciare and the other actresses, who were screaming in rage and fear while they struggled and lashed out with foot and hand. Androv and the two other greybeards of the company were already stretched unmoving on the ground.

Coll roared with anger and charged straight at the soldier who held Ciare around the waist. His spear struck the man in the buttock; the soldier howled, dropping Ciare to clap a hand over his wound, then saw Coll raising his spear again and yanked out a huge dagger.

Ciare caught up a stick and struck him in the face.

The soldier howled and dropped his knife. Coll swung the butt of his staff, cracking it against the man's forehead, and the soldier slumped to the ground. Then Coll leaped in front of Ciare, spear raised to guard her. Another soldier came at him, howling rage and swinging a halberd. Coll shot his spear up to block and kicked the man in the stomach, but the axe head ripped his left arm as the soldier doubled over. Coll shouted in anger and swung the butt right into the man's face; he tumbled to the ground and lay still. Coll gave him a quick glance to be sure he wasn't moving as he pulled back on guard.

But there were only three men still standing: Dirk, who stood in the center of four fallen men, his blade naked, eyes alight, chest heaving; Gar, who stood with rapier and dagger ready; and a knight, who hauled himself up from the ground by clinging to stirrup and saddle, then stepped away from his horse and drew his sword. His lance lay broken on the ground.

"I am Sir Lageb of Oxl," the knight called from behind his visor. "Who are you, that I should deign to cross swords with you?"

"Nice excuse," Dirk taunted, but Gar said clearly, "I am Sir Gar Pike."

"Deserter!" the knight shouted, and advanced, cleaver swinging.

Gar parried with his rapier, and the broadsword sliced deep into the turf. As Sir Lageb yanked it free, Gar wound up a ferocious figure-eight swing, cut low in a feint and, as Sir Lageb dropped his hilt to block, swung high to clash his rapier into the knight's helmet so hard that it rang. Sir Lageb stumbled back, then fell. Gar dropped to one knee beside him, tore his gorget loose and his helmet off, then swung a short hard stroke with the hilt of his dagger. Sir Lageb went limp.

"Yes," Gar mused, "he does look familiar."

"He'll feel better when we tell him we were trying to come back, but got delayed," Dirk assured him. "Uh . . . Coll?"

"Later, if you please, Master Dirk." Coll held Ciare sobbing into his shoulder, his eyes closed, face a study in bliss.

Dirk grinned and turned back to Gar, but the big man was already stopping over Master Androv, splashing water on his face. Dirk turned to help one of the other greybeards, but Dicea threw herself into his arms first.

"It's done now," Dirk soothed. "It'll be all right."

"But they have taken Enrico!" Dicea wailed.

Dirk stilled. "Enrico?" He exchanged a glance of relief with Gar, who turned back to Master Androv; the player chief was already trying to get up.

"Not so fast," the giant advised. "Take a drink, then tell me what happed to Enrico—and, now that I look, all your other young men."

"Not to mention your other cart," Dirk added.

"Need you ask?" Androv said bitterly. "Soldiers!"

Gar nodded. "The king pressed your young men into his army?"

"Nay—Duke Trangray! He has marched his whole army

to the border of Earl Insol's estates, and is gathering every man he can find to throw against His Majesty's spears!"

Dicea gave out a keening cry.

"Must be some way to stop the battle," Dirk offered.

"None ever have," Androv said grimly.

"And your cart?"

"At least they threw our trunks and properties out before they took it and the oxen that drew it. They took one ox from this cart, too, and told us they were being generous to leave us so much! We pressed on to seek sanctuary with the king, but you see what has come of that—his soldiers came to take our last ox for food and our actresses for their pleasure!"

"Which they have not, praise you young men!" Mama came tottering up to throw her arms about her son. "However did you know we needed you?"

Dirk looked up, startled, then turned to Gar. "Good question. How *did* we know?"

"Simply good fortune," Gar assured him.

"*Just* good fortune?"

"Well, perhaps a little bird told me."

"Yeah, the little bird who sits in your brain!"

Coll would have wondered at that, but he was too much occupied with the two women who meant the world to him.

Ciare finally managed to pull a little away from Coll, gasping away the last of her tears. "I was so frightened! Oh, thank Heaven you came in time, Coll!"

"Thank Heaven indeed," he agreed fervently. "Oh, I have so worried about you, Ciare!"

"Worried?" Ciare stared. "After the way I scolded and shouted at you? How could you still care?"

Coll caught her hand tightly in his own, looking deeply into her eyes, and said, "How could I not?"

Ciare still stared at him, then lowered her gaze, blushing. "I—I was so much a shrew! I have cursed myself far worse than ever I scolded you! Oh, forgive me, Coll!"

"I think he already has." Mama smiled, amused, then turned away to soothe the other older women.

"There is nothing to forgive," Coll told her gravely. "I wronged you horribly. We brought danger upon you all, and I could at least have told you."

"Not without breaking faith with your masters." Ciare looked up into his eyes again. "I saw that later. But I didn't think at the time; I only knew that I was very, very hurt. And here you come charging in to save me from three times your number! Oh, Coll, I can't even be angry with your masters now, and certainly not with you!"

"I should have told you anyway." Coll gathered her in, holding her and savoring the feel of her next to him. "I should have told you."

Dirk had to turn from comforting Dicea as one of the soldiers stirred. He dropped down to one knee, dagger poised to strike the man's head again, but the soldier only squinted painfully up at him and pleaded, "Hold your hand, I pray you, sir knight! You strike hard indeed!"

"Not if I don't have to," Dirk said in a warning tone.

"You don't," the man assured him. He touched the bump on his head gingerly, gasped. "You're a mill of battle."

Dirk went completely still, though he was poised for action. "Like the mills of the gods?"

"No," the soldier said. "You grind your enemies quickly. The mills of the gods grind slowly."

"But they grind exceedingly small," Dirk breathed. He stared at the man a moment longer, then sheathed his dagger and called, "Gar? You'd better come over here."

The soldiers had gathered up their knight and were marching back to the castle beside his horse, six of them carrying the meat of the butchered ox; at Dirk's insistence, they had even paid for it from the knight's purse. Gar and Dirk were discussing their little surprise. Coll overheard, and it made sense to him later, but at the time, it was just part of the wondrous music of the forest all about him, birdsong and windsong and the murmurs of the players as they gathered up their belongings and stowed them once again in the cart.

"Remember the soldiers we talked to, after the show?" Dirk asked.

"In which town?" Gar returned.

Dirk shrugged. "Any one you want—or, more to the point, all of them. Seems they listened better than we thought. They went right back to their platoons and set up cells!"

"But how did they make contact with other cells outside the armies?"

"Just repeated the password until somebody gave the countersign, I guess. Frankly, I don't really care about the why of it anywhere nearly as much as I care about there being cells in both armies."

"He claims the king's army is fairly riddled with them," Gar said, musing, "and that at least half of Duke Trangray's men are pledged to the uprising."

"Just how big an uprising are we planning, Gar?"

"Whatever's necessary." Gar shrugged. "A dukedom or two . . . or three, or ten . . . the royal demesne . . ."

"The whole country, you mean."

"Yes, and let's hope it carries from Aggrand to other lands. This is, after all, only one kingdom, and not a very big one at that. Seeds are small, though."

"Sir Gar?"

They looked up; Master Androv was coming up to them. "Yes, Master Androv!" Gar stood, towering over the chief player. "My apologies, my deepest apologies, for having embroiled you in our rabble-rousing. I should have realized it might bring trouble upon you."

"You've certainly made up for it now." Androv gestured

at the cart. "You preserved what little the first batch of soldiers left us."

"It was the least I could do," Gar said. "But what did you come to say?"

"Only that we're ready to set out again, and to thank you for your help." Androv held out a hand.

Gar took it. "But they've taken all your oxen! How will you move the cart?"

"There's still some strength left in our old bones," Androv said, "and if we all pull together, I fancy a dozen players can do what one ox did."

"Nonsense!" Gar brushed the notion aside. "We have horses, after all. We'll harness them to the traces and pull your wagon for you."

Alarm filled Androv's face. "No, no, sir, you need not!"

"Yes, I do. We must make recompense in full for our earlier misdeeds! Come on, Dirk! Bring your horse!" And Gar strode away to untie his mount and bring it to the front of the cart.

"No, no, Sir Gar, really!" Androv came running after him, palms upheld to halt him. "We can manage, sir, we can manage!"

"With great diffculty, maybe." Gar stopped and turned to him with a smile. "You're afraid we're going to use your troupe to disguise our subversion, aren't you?"

"Well . . . we couldn't ask you to forgo something so important to you . . ." Androv said weakly.

"Of course you could, and should! Don't worry, Master Androv—one spy has caught us with you, so more spies will be listening wherever we go. I'm not promising that I won't say anything about an uprising to anyone, mind you—but I do promise that I'll be much more discreet. Besides, the time for talking has passed, and the time for action is almost upon us!" He turned away to unsaddle his horse, leaving Master Androv looking more alarmed than before.

Still, he couldn't really stop a couple of knights from escorting his company if they insisted. They harnessed the horses to the cart, then pulled it out of the woodlot and along the road, Gar and Dirk walking beside with their hands on their swords, keeping watch all about them, giving every hedgerow, cottage, and byre a suspicious glare, no matter how innocent it seemed.

As for Coll, he walked beside the cart, too, but only had eyes for Ciare, who beamed down at him from her seat above. He tripped and barely recovered his balance a dozen times, but he still could only stare at her. Dicea leaned down to hiss at him, "Coll! You're making a fool of yourself in front of the whole troupe!" But he only shook his head and grinned, amazed at how happy he could be just to walk beside the cart, gazing up at the woman he loved and occasionally touching her hand.

The attack had delayed them, so darkness caught them in open farmland. They pulled the cart off the road and pitched camp, with the men rolling their blankets up against a hedgerow. The women slept under the cart in case of rain—and the older women pointedly made sure Ciare slept in the center.

They woke at first light, and were just setting a pot to boil over the campfire when they heard a drum roll and a trumpet blow, then heard the yelling and clashing break out nearby. Everyone turned to stare—except Dirk, Gar, and Androv.

"Quickly, into the carts!" the chief player called, and shooed them all up to their perches. They complained that they hadn't had breakfast, to which he replied, "Be glad you have your lives!" Gar smothered the fire, then ran to help Dirk harness the horses to the shafts.

The cart rumbled back onto the road. Dirk shook the reins, calling to them, and the horses kicked into a trot.

"No faster, I pray," Androv shouted to him, "or they'll spill all of us!"

Dirk nodded, face rigid, and held the horses at the trot.

Shouting and clashing broke out on the other side of the road, too, and they saw troops in strange livery running toward them—or rather, toward the battle line beyond; they just happened to be in the way.

"Whose colors are those?" Dirk called.

"Earl Trangray!" Coll called back.

"Impatient, isn't he?" Gar asked. "He just couldn't wait for the rest of the dukes to arrive!"

"Maybe he's only feeling out the situation, to see how strong the king is," Dirk yelled back.

"The more fool he, then!"

Coll was amazed how sure he sounded, and even more amazed at the firmness of Gar's nod of agreement.

Then an arrow flew from the left edge of the road and sank into the side of Dirk's horse. The beast screamed, rearing; then its knees folded, and it fell, dead. The other plowed to a halt and the cart bucked; the players screamed as it almost overturned. Coll threw himself across to the far side, and it settled back—just in time for a spear to come hurtling from the right side of the road and sink deeply into the chest of Gar's horse. The poor beast dropped without a sound.

Dirk cursed as he leaped down, drawing his sword to chop through the harness. Gar did the same, while Dirk raged, "I'll kill them! I'll draw and quarter them! Poor beast! What did *he* ever do to them?"

"Got in their way," Gar called, "and so did we! Haul! Put your back into it! Before they reach the road!"

Each man grabbed a trace and threw himself against the weight of the wagon. Coll leaped down to join them, and so did Master Androv and the two older men, though more slowly. They all grabbed hold of the tongue and heaved. Slowly, the cart ground into motion, then began to roll. The dead horses passed between the wheels, and the players were on their way to safety.

Coll was amazed at how smoothly and easily the cart

went, seeming to grow lighter with every step. Soon they were all trotting, beginning to breathe hard.

"We have it going now!" Gar called. "Everyone over thirty, drop out and jog along!"

The older men did, thankfully, and Gar, Dirk, and Coll pulled the cart by themselves. They were a hundred yards down the road before the troops broke onto it, halberd clashing against pike with roaring and shouting, knights riding through it all laying about them with their swords.

Then a dozen soldiers leaped onto the road before the players, leveling spears, and a knight rode up behind them, crying, "Halt!" Then he saw Gar and howled, "It's the deserter! You have heard of him, everyone has heard of him! And the players are harboring him! Slay them all!"

14

A re you out of your mind, man?" Gar stormed. "These
are civilians, and there's a battle coming right toward
us! Let them pass!"

"Them, perhaps, but not you!" The knight spurred his
horse and charged down at Gar. Coll, in a panic, caught up
his spear. Gar leaped aside, and the knight thundered on
alongside the cart, trying to turn his horse. Coll leaned out,
bracing his spear. It caught the knight right under the chin
of his helm, and he reeled in the saddle. Gar leaped to hug
the man around the middle and haul him down from his
saddle. The knight hit the ground with more clang than
thud.

Androv turned ashen. "You're a dead man, Coll!"

"I've been dead for five months now," Coll retorted. "I
still manage to get a lot done." Inside, though, his stomach
sank. It was indeed death for a serf to strike a knight.

The soldiers knew that, too; they shouted in anger and
charged.

Dirk leaped into their path, catching one man's spear
on his dagger and another on his sword. The parries threw
the spears up, and their balance off; with quick kicks, he

sent them reeling into the men behind them. Gar stepped in to take two more, but a third thrust a spear right at his face; he managed to dodge, but the soldier slammed into him, and down he went. The soldier lifted his spear high and thrust down with all his might, but Gar rolled aside, then up to his feet, and swung at the man while he was still trying to wrestle his spear out of the ground. The soldier had sense enough to let go, duck, and come in to slam a punch into Gar's jaw. Gar reeled back, and another soldier stuck out a spear to trip him. Gar fell, and the soldier kicked him twice, hard.

Coll shouted, leaping down, and charged.

He caught the soldier in the shoulder just as he managed to yank his spear free. Gar came to his feet in time to catch the other soldier, hefting him high to hurl him into the faces of the two remaining soldiers who came running, spears leveled.

"Remaining" because, with Gar and Coll having tied up four soldiers, Dirk had managed to knock out the rest. Several lay clutching their heads and moaning; others just lay, period. Gar limped up to him, breathing hard. "Well done."

"*Ill* done," Dirk snapped. "One of them will never move again!"

"Better him than us," Gar wheezed, "and they weren't in a mood to be particular about what they did to us, or why."

A little life came back into Dirk's face, and Gar turned to clap Coll on the shoulder. "Thank you, Coll—twice. This knight would have spitted me on his lance if it hadn't been for you, and his man would have done the same." He turned to the knight, knelt, and lifted his visor. Bleary eyes opened and looked up at him, then snapped wide in horror.

"Tell the king you were felled by Sir Gar Pike," Gar told him, "whose squire saved him from your cowardly onslaught. No, no excuses—if you knew enough to call me a deserter, you knew who I was. Now, thanks to my man, I can slog onward, trying to return to my king."

"I—I had not known," the knight stammered.

"You knew very well, and your eagerness to kill me must make us wonder for whom you truly fight. Still, I'll say nothing about this unfortunate 'mistake' if you don't. I've too many other things to worry me, such as defeating the alliance of lords. I leave you your life—but I will take your horse, since you slew mine."

Outrage flared in the knight's eyes, but he was in no position to argue. "It is the least I can do to atone for my error," he said stiffly.

"I thank you," Gar said gravely. "We shall return him to you when we have found our king again. Until then, farewell. Coll, prop him up against a tree."

Dirk had to help him, but they managed to wrestle the knight over to a tree where he could lean back. By the time they were done, Gar had lashed the horse to the tongue of the cart, using his saddle cinch and one of the reins. The cart ground into motion, leaving behind a knight who was struggling to his feet by leaning heavily on a tree.

With the horse to help and Dirk, Gar, and Coll to help the horse, they finally managed to haul the cart up into the shelter of a rocky outcrop. Gar began to curry the poor beast and assure it how noble it was, while Elspeth took a leather bucket to a nearby spring to draw water for it.

Dirk wiped his brow. "You know, it occurs to me that we could have saved a lot of effort by leaving the cart."

"True," Androv wheezed, "but the properties and stage are our livelihood, Sir Dirk. Without it, we might be able to earn a living by pantomimes on fair days—or we might not."

Dirk nodded. "Okay, I guess we do have to take it along.

Besides, we can always hide under it if the battle catches up with us again."

It did exactly that only an hour later—or its aftermath did.

Suddenly there were soldiers falling all about them as they leaped down from the hilltop above. Some still held spears, but most were fleeing in outright panic. They struck at the players, bawling their fright, then ran on down the slope.

"Back! As far under the brow of the hill as you can!" Gar shouted. Elspeth took the horse's reins and led the charger back into cover, then cowered beside it while Gar beat fleeing soldiers away and Dirk and Coll threw their weight against the cart, trundling it back until it jarred against rock. They turned it sideways, so that falling soldiers wouldn't snap the tongue, then took up positions around it, ready to defend. They only had to push away the occasional soldier, though.

"Why are they in such a panic?" Coll called to Gar.

"Because their side lost," Gar answered. "Now they're running for their lives."

"Then the king has won," Coll cried, "for those are Duke Trangray's colors!"

"He should have waited for the rest of the dukes, after all," Dirk said, grinning.

"The losers don't bother me," Gar told them. "They'll only attack us if we get in their way. It's the winners I'm worried about."

"Yeah." Dirk turned grim, sword and dagger out and at rest, but ready to snap up to guard. "Victors look for loot—and since there's no town nearby, we're the closest thing."

They kept on fending off fleeing soldiers till the color of the livery suddenly changed. King's men leaped off the brow of the hill, chasing the duke's soldiers, and more of them came running around the side of the outcrop. They saw the players and skidded to a halt, grinning. "Loot! Are you fool enough to try to keep us from it?"

"I am," Gar said grimly. "We're knights, and this is our squire."

"They got women in there?" one ranker asked, pushing toward the cart—then stopping as Dirk's rapier circled in front of his stomach. "Hey, now! Get aside and let us at 'em, or we'll bury you under men!"

"Some of you will be killed," Gar warned him. "Want to be the first?"

The soldier glared at him, but didn't answer. Gar waited. But while he did, more and more soldiers assembled behind the first one. "What's to do, Dool?"

"The big one says they're knights, but they don't look like it—and they got women in there and they won't let us at 'em!"

"Women?"

"Hit 'em!"

"Bury 'em!"

The king's men roared and rushed.

Coll caught a spear on his shaft, thrust it high, and clipped the soldier with the butt. The man fell, but two more pressed in in his place. Coll swung, slashing and striking, feeling blades cut his arms and legs, determined to keep them from Ciare. Beside him, Dirk and Gar thrust and cut and parried, and king's men fell before them. Then a pike butt cracked into Coll's jaw and he fell back against the cart. Dimly, he heard men roaring, heard Gar bellow with anger, and heard a series of loud thuds. Then he could see again, but the world seemed to tilt around him. It steadied, showing a dozen men lying on the ground before Dirk and Gar, who were both breathing heavily, both striped with blood from cuts on forehead, cheek, and arm—but the king's men held their distance, uncertain.

Then a knight rode around the side of the outcrop and cried, "What moves?"

"They say they're knights," a soldier wheezed.

The visored helm turned toward Gar. "*Whose* knights?"

"The king's," Gar panted. "I'm Sir Gar Pike, and this is Sir Dirk Dulaine."

Everyone froze.

Then the knight threw his visor up. "Where in hell have *you* two been?"

"Not in hell, but here and there about the countryside," Gar said, still panting. "We were cut off from the king's troops, retreated running and fighting, and found ourselves way behind enemy lines. We hid in the greenwood, and have been trying to work our way back to His Majesty ever since."

"Nay!" A soldier shoved his way to the front and pointed a shaking finger at Gar. "He's the one who unhorsed Sir Bricbald and left him for dead! Left the rest of us, too!"

"Ah, yes," Gar drawled. "I seem to recognize this soldier's readiness to fight three men when he had a dozen on his side!"

The soldier reddened. "A deserter Sir Bricbald named him, and a deserter he is!"

Coll lunged at the man with his spear, but Gar caught his shoulder and held him back.

"Him, too!" The soldier leaped away, pointing now at Coll. "All three of them! Deserters, all! And these players have harbored them!"

"I find it hard to believe that a knight who was so close an adviser to the king would desert," the knight said slowly, "but if Sir Bricbald laid the charge, we must consider it with some weight."

"Weight!" Gar said in disgust. "He only repeated a charge he had heard a soldier make—a soldier who had fled the battle himself!"

"He did not!" the accusing soldier said hotly.

Gar turned to him, recognition coming into his eyes. "Perhaps I *do* know you . . ."

"Enough!" the knight cried. "Sir Gar and Sir Dirk, if you are truly guiltless, as I suspect, I will ask your pardon— but until then, we must take you before the king, and let him decide."

"Excellent!" Gar lowered sword and dagger and straightened. "That's where I've been trying to go, anyway!"

Well, Coll knew that wasn't what Gar had really been trying to do, and so did Dirk—but who else? Certainly not the players. Oh, several dozen prisoners, sixty forest outlaws, and a whole grab bag of young aristocrats, soldiers, and merchants who had come to see the plays—but he doubted anyone was about to ask them.

"But we cannot leave these good players, who have been so hospitable to us, without defense," Gar told the knight. "They must come along, and under my care, too."

"If you say it, they shall," the knight agreed, "and you and Sir Dirk shall of course keep your swords in your hands. You shall not need them, though." That last was said in a tone of iron, as he swept his soldiers with a threatening glance. A murmur of assent passed through their ranks, and spears lowered.

So they went, with a very relieved Master Androv driving, and Coll aboard the cart comforting a sobbing Ciare. Dicea glanced at them, and longing was naked in her face; then she turned away, somehow looking gaunt and hollow-eyed. Coll's heart went out to his sister. Was it only because he and Ciare had what Dicea wanted? Or was there something more? He decided to ask Mama as soon as there was a moment's rest.

Gar and Dirk strode in front of the cart, so Coll didn't hear Dirk saying, very softly, "I could see the doubt rising in him the moment you started talking, and the decision you wanted coming right behind it. You weren't working on him with words alone, were you?"

"Come now, Dirk!" Gar smiled. "Would I do a thing like that? Surely sweet reason is enough to convince any man!"

"What's sweet about it?" Dirk grumbled. "No, don't say it—you could only answer with a psi."

They came to a town miraculously untouched by the war, perhaps because it stood at the farthest border of Insol's estates—or perhaps because it had high, strong walls, with stout oaken gates. Those gates stood open at the moment, and the knight drew the procession to a halt. "Your player folk will be safe here, and may even earn some gold."

Gar nodded. "We must leave them, then."

Coll looked up in alarm, then leaped down from the cart, but Gar was already reaching up to shake Master Androv's hand. "I thank you for your hospitality, sir. May you fare well. If we can, we'll summon you to play for the king when we've won."

"Optimist," Dirk muttered.

Gar turned to Coll. "Make your good-byes, for we must go, and quickly."

"Good-bye again?" Ciare blazed. "Why, you lack-love, you summer suitor! Have you no faithfulness at all?"

"My love, I have no choice!" Coll protested.

"Absolutely none," the knight agreed, his tone once more iron. "He goes to the king for judgment."

"Judgment! Aye, and even if His Majesty judges you guiltless, will I see you again? Not likely! You have had what you seek, and go to seek more!"

"I will come back . . ."

"Aye, when you've emptied your heart to some other lass! Then you'll come to me to fill it again! But do not, sir, for I'll be gone! A deserter they have named you, and a deserter you are—but you haven't deserted the king, you've deserted *me!*" And she burst into tears as she turned away.

Coll stared after her, dumbstruck, but his mother reached down to pat his shoulder. "It's her grief that's talking, son, not her reason—grief at losing you, grief that she must join your sister now in the agony of waiting and hoping her man will return alive and well."

"My sister!" Coll stared up at her. "What man does she await?" Then he cursed himself for saying it aloud, and glanced at Dirk and Gar.

"No, not them," Mama said. "While you were gone, she fell in love with young Enrico, the player who does the simpletons so well."

Coll stared, then felt joy begin in his heart, joy for his sister at the same time that he felt an echo of his own sense of loss, aching in sympathy with hers. "They took him for a soldier!"

"They did, so if your friends can really end this war as swiftly as they think, tell them to do it! Before Enrico gets killed." She transferred her hand to his head. "Go with my blessing, son. We'll do our best to look after your Ciare for you."

"And I'll look after Enrico, if I can find him! Thank you, Mother—and God be with you!"

Earl Insol's great hall wasn't much less imposing than the king's, and the king was just as impressive as he had been, and no more. Coll decided the youngster hadn't learned much from this campaign. He was astonished to realize that he felt older than the king, and was actually looking at His Majesty as something of a silly man!

"Sir Gar." The king's tone was carefully neutral. "It is long since I have seen you."

"Too long indeed, sire." Gar had already bowed. "We

were separated from your army in the fighting—pursued Earl Insol's troops too hard, and became lost behind his lines. We didn't know he had lost, so we hid in the greenwood, and have been working our way back to you ever since."

"Such loyalty is to be commended." But His Majesty didn't issue the commendation, and carefully didn't say whether or not he believed Gar. He didn't seem to want to press the issue, though.

Gar pegged the reason. "I am delighted to see Duke Trangray's sally so easily put to flight. Has the battle plan worked well, then?"

Now Coll understood that even before Earl Insol's attack, Gar had left the king instructions for repelling an attack by another lord.

"Perfectly! It could not have fared better if you had read Trangray's mind." But the king frowned. "How could you know it was he who would attack me?"

"I did not," Gar said frankly, "but I knew the lords couldn't let this challenge to their power go unanswered. The more distant lords might, but the closer lords wouldn't dare, because you might try to set your law upon them."

The king's eye gleamed. "They would judge rightly!"

"Indeed," Gar agreed. "There was a chance they might league together—but even if they did, the first to arrive at your new borders would grow impatient, and test your strength with a small part of his forces."

"So, of course, you advised me to answer with a major portion of my own! But you did not know it would be Duke Trangray?"

"I didn't," Gar replied. "I knew it would be a duke, who could call up the forces of all his earls, for you had already proved you could beat the forces of one earl alone. And I knew it would be one of the nearer dukes rather than one of the farther. But I could not know it would be Trangray."

"You knew well enough!" The king was regaining some

enthusiasm. "And have you learned nothing more for me, while you were 'lost'?"

All those weeks with the players had at least taught Gar how to take a cue. "I have learned that Trangray has sent to all the dukes to league with him in attacking Your Majesty, and that four have said they will come; moreover, rumor has it that they march already. But your spies have surely told you as much."

"They have told me that four dukes march toward me," the king replied, "but they haven't told me that Trangray summoned them to an alliance! How did you learn this, Sir Gar?"

Gar shrugged. "Rumor has many tongues, Your Majesty."

"Yes, and you seem to speak them all! But tell me now, Sir Gar: How shall we go about whipping these arrogant dukes home, eh? For surely, their forces must outnumber mine by ten to one!"

"Seven to one, if Rumor speaks truth," Gar told him, "though I have found that Rumor's estimates grow as they travel. Probably he will have only five men to your one—but it won't hurt us to plan on seven." He glanced about him. "Beyond that, I'm reluctant to speak more without seeing Your Majesty's maps, and learning all that your spies have told you."

The king was no genius, but he was shrewd; he took the hint that, with twenty guards and soldiers plus a dozen courtiers, there might very well be spies of Duke Trangray's listening. He nodded. "Away to my solar, then! Knights, you may leave us! Sir Gar, come!" He turned to go.

Gar stepped quickly to follow, and Coll and Dirk jumped to catch up. The King's bodyguard gathered around them. Gar turned to give a wave of thanks to the knight who had brought them in. Bemused, the knight waved back.

Up the stairs they went, and swept into the solar, lately

Earl Insol's—but his escutcheon had been removed, and the king's installed. A bank of tall windows opened onto the courtyard, spreading light over a map of the kingdom. His Majesty stepped behind the table and pointed down, looking up at Gar—then stared at Coll. "What is this common soldier doing here?"

"He is my sergeant," Gar explained, "and serves me in place of a squire. He must know everything I know, or he cannot serve me well. He is as trustworthy as Sir Dirk himself."

Dirk bowed his head in acknowledgment of the praise. But Coll noticed that Gar hadn't said just how far Dirk was to be trusted. The former serf was learning subtlety.

15

The planning session droned on, and Coll's attention wandered—to Ciare, of course. Unwise—thinking of her raised an ache in him, of loss and grief. The way she had raged at him, she was surely lost to him forever! Of course, it could be that Mama had been right, that Ciare had only flared with the moment's anger, and would realize that he was still devoted to her and would come back as soon as he was . . .

"Coll."

He jolted out of his trance, blinked, and focused on Dirk's face. "Outside," the knight told him. "You're not doing any good for us here, and even less for yourself. Go circulate among the soldiers and see if you can pick up any . . . news."

Coll stared back at him, wondering about the emphasis on the last word. Then it struck him—Dirk meant for him to find out if there were any cells here, in the castle! Coll nodded. "As you wish, Master Dirk." He turned away, and the guards, frowning, opened the door to let him out.

Purpose thrilled through him now, keeping him from brooding, though he had to work hard to keep Ciare from his thoughts. He asked servants twice for directions to the door and finally found himself in the courtyard.

It was a hive of activity. A metallic tattoo rang out from the forges against the eastern wall, where a dozen smiths beat iron into blades and spear points; wagons rolled to and from the granary, with oats and hay for horses and wheat for the kitchens, which belched smoke and wafted the smell of roasting meat over the courtyard. Servants scurried back and forth on a dozen errands, and groups of soldiers practiced archery and spear drill in the center of the yard, while other groups lounged around them, watching and waiting for their turns.

That was Coll's goal. He threaded his way between running servants, jumped out of the way of rumbling carts, and came up behind the soldiers. For a while, he did nothing more than wander from group to group, listening to the eternal soldiers' griping. Then he began to join in—you could always talk about how bad the food was, and the weather, and the officers. He chatted with a dozen different soldiers before he struck up a conversation with a sergeant consisting of guesses about what the cooks used to do for a living before they joined the army. "We had one that must have been a mason," he told one group. "At least, his bread was hard as rock."

The soldier nodded. "I know what you mean. We had one who must have been a charcoal burner, to judge by what he did to our meat."

Coll laughed. "Of course, our cook said it wasn't his fault—that no one could have made soft bread from the grain he was given. He said it was so hard that only the mills of the gods could have ground it into flour."

There was an edge to the soldier's laugh—or did Coll only imagine it? The sergeant turned easily to watch the rest of his friends step up to take their places at practice. "Come on, Galwin!" another sergeant called.

"Not just yet," Galwin called back. His mates shrugged

and turned to swipe at one another. "Even if you could get that grain to the mills of the gods," Galwin said, "you'd wait a long, long time for your flour."

Coll's whole system seemed to leap into higher speed. "Yes, because the mills of the gods grind slowly."

"But they grind exceedingly small," the sergeant returned. They exchanged a knowing, wary glance, then turned back to watch the practice and stood silent for several minutes.

"So what do you have to tell me?" Galwin asked.

"Nothing to tell," Coll returned. "Only to ask. How many cells are there in the king's army?"

"Almost half." Galwin didn't even have to stop to think about it.

"Is there any contact with the armies of the dukes?"

The soldier nodded. "A peasant came in this morning to sell vegetables. He says that almost all of Duke Trangray's men are with us, and at least a third of the armies of each of the other dukes."

Coll stood for a moment, amazed. Admittedly, they had been building this movement for four months, but still, it had happened with amazing speed. "Thank you," he said. "I'll come watch practice now and again."

"You'd better be part of it, or the knights will wonder at your coming," the sergeant advised.

"Good idea. Let's try."

Galwin nodded and stepped out to join the practice bout. Coll borrowed a wooden-headed spear from another man and went with him.

It felt good to strive against another man without worrying about killing or being killed. Coll learned a few tricks and taught the sergeant some, then clapped him on the back in thanks, thanked all the other soldiers for letting him join their practice, and came back to the keep just as Dirk and Gar were coming out, their faces expressionless.

That woodenness made Coll brace himself. "Did the planning go well?"

"Very well," Gar assured him. "I need to survey the defenses, though. Let's walk about a while."

Coll understood, and fell in beside Gar. The only way they could be sure they wouldn't be overheard was to be out in the open—and busy as it was, the courtyard was huge enough that they could be sure no one was near.

Gar angled over toward the wall, but stayed fifty feet away from it. "What have you learned?"

"That almost half the king's army is with us," Coll told him, "and most of Duke Trangray's army. The other dukes have a third of their men at least, who will act when we say."

"So many?" Dirk turned to stare at him. "In just four months?"

"We chose the right men." Gar nodded, pleased. "And we seem to have come at a time when many, many people are ready to jump to anything that gives them hope."

"Oh, yes," Coll assured him. "When your father and grandfather have been ground down by war, and you've spent most of your life nearly starving? Oh, yes. My people will lunge at any trace of hope you offer. But the dukes still have more men than we have."

"Right." Dirk nodded. "A third of each army is good, but it's not enough."

"It will have to be." Gar's voice hardened again. "You know what they mean to do, Dirk—kill off half their armies trying to beat the king back, then crack his castle and shell him out."

Dirk gave a grim nod. "And the king is more than willing to let them kill most of his soldiers, as long as he kills more of theirs."

Coll stared in horror. "Who will win?"

"There's no way of knowing," Gar told him, "but we can be sure that the soldiers will lose. A third of each army will have to do. We can't wait for more, or there won't be enough living men to bury the dead. I wish I hadn't helped the king win that first battle. If they'd beaten him back then, they wouldn't be ready to massacre each other now!''

"Yes, but there would have been no check on the dukes, and no way to make them stop their constant petty wars,'' Dirk reminded.

"Yes!'' Coll said fervently. "If we're not all killed tomorrow, we will be next year, or the year after! Any chance is worth taking, Master Gar!''

"Then we'll have to take it,'' the big knight said grimly. "The cells will have to begin by knocking out their fellow soldiers while they sleep, then tying them down. Even then, there will be battles with the dukes' bodyguards, and they'll have to starve the lords out of their keeps!''

But, "No,'' Coll said. "Serfs do the lords' work for them, so serfs know all the ways into and out of a keep. Rest assured, Master Gar—the soldiers can be sure someone will leave a door open, before the bodyguard knows they're needed.''

"Then that's how it will have to be,'' Gar said. "Knock out the soldiers loyal to the dukes, then hold the noblemen themselves prisoners—but don't kill them, or there will be no hope at all of peace! The oldest sergeant in each army is in command, the second oldest after him, and so on down the ages and the ranks! Go chat with your new acquaintances, Coll, and tell them to spread the word: the egg will hatch at first light on Twoday!''

"But that's only five days!'' Dirk protested. "They can't possibly spread the word that fast!''

"They'll have to. The spies say the other four dukes will arrive late Monday or early Tuesday, and the battle will begin on Wednesday. We don't dare let them all get together before the serfs rise. Ready or not, the egg must hatch!''

But Dirk shook his head. "Even cell communication isn't *that* fast. Face it, Gar—you're going to have to bring in the Wizard after all."

"I suppose I knew this was coming all along," Gar sighed. "Well, if that's all he has to do, I suppose I should be happy."

Coll, overhearing, went into a superstitious sweat. Could they really mean it? Did they really know a wizard? And would he really be willing to help? No, impossible!

But that night, he had no sooner lain down in his bunk than a face appeared in the darkness, an old face surrounded by billowing white hair that merged into a swirling white beard. *I am the Wizard of War!* a deep voice rumbled inside his head.

Coll went stiff, staring into the night, petrified.

Fear not—the war I wage is yours! I will not hurt you.

"But you'll make sure we don't lose?" Coll asked, hope surging.

I cannot promise that, though I will do what I can to help. Still, it is you serfs who must do the fighting yourselves. What I can do, I shall—for now, spreading word of the time and day the egg must hatch.

"Can you really?" Coll breathed, amazed. "Can you really tell every member of every cell?"

Even I cannot do that. But I can tell one leader in each demesne, and I can take the most urgent messages from one man to another. You are the man I have chosen for the king's demesne.

Coll shrank from the responsibility. "No! I'm only a serf, only a man who waits on other men!"

Some serfs will have to become commanders, or you shall always be pawns at the mercy of the lords. You are the serf Sir Dirk and Sir Gar have chosen to know the strategy and tactics of this War against Wars, so it is you who must shepherd all the cells and be sure they will all act together. I can be only a helper in this; it must be a man of Aggrand who directs the battle, or your people will al-

ways be serfs who obey another's bidding and wait for a rescuer to come take them from their misery.

"I'm not able enough! I'm ignorant, I'm humble!"

So are you all, Coll. What, would you rather I talk with a sergeant?

"Yes! Uh . . ." Coll remembered that he *was* a sergeant now, Gar's sergeant. "I see. If I want the rank, I have to do the work, is that it?"

Part of what you must want, yes.

"And if I want to be free, I must win freedom myself?"

You, and all your people, the wizard confirmed. *If another does it for you, another can take it from you.*

"Which is to say that if someone else frees me, I can never really be free." Coll steeled himself to the notion. "All right, I will spread the word. 'The egg will hatch at first light on Twoday.' "

In the dead of night, a dozen of Earl Gripard's soldiers climbed out of their bunks and, moving silently on bare feet, struck their sleeping comrades on their heads, then bound the unconscious men to their bunks with strong rope. The same thing happened in every other barracks; then the men came out, shod but still moving quietly, to surround the Earl's tent. A grizzled sergeant and five soldiers marched up to the door flap. The sentries frowned, but didn't raise weapons. "What's to do?" one asked.

"Forgive us, brothers," the sergeant said, and his men leaped forward to knock out their former companions.

The first rays of sunlight struck the side of the tent, and the earl awoke. Yawning, he pulled on his dressing gown and came out to view the morning—and saw two-thirds of his army bound hand and foot, with the other third guarding them. "What is the meaning of this?" he bawled. "Sergeant! Untie those men!"

The sergeant bowed and said, very courteously, "My apologies, my lord, but we will not!"

The earl stared at him in shock. Then his face swelled, and he turned to his door guards. "Seize that man!"

"Your pardon, my lord." The door guard to the left bowed. "But in this matter, I will obey only my sergeant."

The earl stared again, shocked anew. Then he lifted his head and bellowed, "Sir Godfrey! Sir Arthur! Teach these arrogant villeins their proper places!"

"Your knights, too, are bound and under guard," the sergeant informed him. "They cannot come to do your bidding!"

The earl rounded on the sergeant. "What is the meaning of this!"

"Only that we shall obey you in all else, my lord," the sergeant said, "but we will not fight this war."

In a castle two hundred miles away, at the border of Aggrand, two-thirds of the army lay trussed like turkeys; only a few were beginning to come to with splitting headaches as a door opened at the base of the keep, and soldiers moved silently in. The kitchens were dark, for there was scarcely even twilight outside. Nonetheless, a single lamp was lit. The soldiers passed in, their boots seeming loud on the stones. They climbed the stairs as quietly as they could, but the sentries at the duke's bedchamber heard them coming and braced their spears, crying, "Hold! Who goes there?"

Figures sprang from the stairwell, silent, stabbing. The sentries howled "Murder!" even as they parried one spear after another, howled and howled until steel thudded through their chests and into the doorjambs. They died, but the rest of the bodyguard came boiling out. The fighting was thick and furious then, but the way was narrow, and though there were only fifty bodyguards, they forced the attackers back into the stairwell.

Then the door of the bedchamber slammed open and

the duke strode out in his robe, calling, "Slay them! Slay every traitorous one of them!"

Then figures rose up behind him—a butler, two footmen, and half a dozen potboys. Hard hands pinioned his arms and a carving knife pressed against his throat. "Guards, throw down your weapons," the butler cried, "or your duke dies!"

The bodyguards froze.

"Throw them down!" the duke cried in a strangled tone.

Slowly, the bodyguards dropped their spears. The soldiers swarmed back up the stairs with coils of rope to tie them fast while the butler and his men took the duke back inside, to seat him in his bedside chair with all due respect—and naked blades. His wife thrust herself back against the headboard, eyes wide in fright, blankets clutched at her throat.

"Peace, my lady," the butler soothed. "No harm shall come to you—so long as you stay in your bed."

Earl Pomeroy had better spies than most. In the dead of night, his soldiers surrounded the revolutionaries, raised spears, and stabbed them dead in their bunks. Then they hauled the dead bodies out into the bailey, to the foot of the stairs that led down from the main door of the keep, where the earl stood, hands on his hips, laughing with vindictive satisfaction. He came down to kick at the bodies, shouting abuse, after which he went back to his bed to sleep soundly, and so did his soldiers.

When they woke, the courtyard was filled with outlaws, and the only soldiers who still lived were tied to their bunks.

Duke Trangray, of course, woke to find himself surrounded by spearpoints, with a white-haired sergeant saying, very courteously, "My lord, we ask that you consider our requests."

The duke went red with fury. He ranted, he raved, he

swore—but the spears never wavered, and under the circumstances, he could hardly refuse.

But less than half isn't enough, and in every barracks, half a dozen soldiers woke to see revolutionaries tying down their comrades. They leaped to their feet, catching up their weapons, and ran bellowing to the attack. Steel rang in every barracks; the fighting spilled out into the courtyard. In two duchies, far from the King's Town, the rebels were conquered and butchered where they stood—but in all others, when the fighting was done, a handful of sergeants presented themselves to their lord, panting, to bow and hear him command, "Slay them all!"

"I regret that we cannot obey you in this, my lord," the oldest sergeant said. "We will obey you in all that is lawful, but we will no longer murder our fellows."

Each lord paled as he realized his loyalists had lost, and that the only soldiers remaining to him were victorious rebels.

The king woke to clamor and saw his own troops fighting one another in the courtyard. Over the battle towered a huge knight in full armor, knocking down any other knight who came near, his back guarded by a smaller armored figure. "Insanity!" swore the king, and called for his own armor. Fully clad and horsed, he rode out to the melee but found the fighting done, except for a cluster of knights who stood at bay, surrounded by a forest of pikes and halberds. The scene was frozen, though; neither knight nor soldier moved.

The huge armored figure rode up to the king, breathing in huge hoarse gasps. The man pushed up his visor and bowed. "Your Majesty," said Sir Gar, "I bring word that the armies of all three dukes are immobilized, and will not fight."

The king's heart sang; in his own army, at least, the loyalists had won! "Seize the opportunity!" he cried. "Attack them one by one, and bring them to me bound in chains!"

"My apologies, Your Majesty," the giant replied, "but I will not fight this war, nor will any of your soldiers who still stand armed."

The king stared, frozen by the magnitude of the realization that in his own army, it was the rebels who had won after all—and that Sir Gar Pike led them!

Then he shouted in fury. "To me! To me, all men of mine!" His bodyguard formed up around their monarch, then followed him into battle, swerving around Sir Gar and striking hard into the forest of pikes. He broke through to his knights, and they rallied to him with a shout. Bellowing, they tore into the throng of serf-soldiers, laying about them with sword and mace, striking down from horseback, not caring whether they hit loyal man or rebel. They didn't notice that one knight after another was falling from his horse until, finally, a space opened around the king as if by magic, and a huge armored form faced him, mounted on a horse as high as his own. Another armored figure rode out beside him, sword and shield upraised, moving toward the few remaining Kings knights.

The knights braced themselves, then charged as one, yelling. But quarterstaves tipped half of them from their saddles as they leaped into motion, and the smaller knight rode to meet the rest, laying about him, parrying cut after cut and counterthrusting while knight after knight fell crashing to the ground. The last two knights suddenly realized what was happening and charged down at Dirk, bellowing. He ducked one thrust and stabbed in under the gorget, then turned to the other knight—just in time for a roundhouse swing to smash into that knight's helmet, toppling him from his saddle. But a soldier leaped up to grab his arm and dragged down, while two others levered him from his saddle. The man fell, crashing.

"Is this your idea of honor, Sir Gar?" the king demanded, his voice thick with fury.

"Your Majesty," the giant said gravely, his voice hollow

within his helmet, "your subjects ask that you listen to their petition."

The king roared with inarticulate fury and spurred his horse. He swung a huge blow with his sword, but Sir Gar caught it on his shield, then caught the next and the next, never returning the blows until the king drew back, panting and trembling, but still furious. "You are no knight! You are a traitor to chivalry!"

"You shall not fight this war," Sir Gar told him.

"Who are you to tell me whether or not I shall attack my dukes!" the king ranted. "You are a foreigner, a ne'er-do-well knight so incompetent that you could not even find a lord to take you into his household, but had to sell your lance instead! Mercenary! Hireling! Who do you think you are?"

"I am Sir Magnus d'Armand," the faceless helm answered. "I am of the line of the Counts d'Armand of Maxima, and the son of Lord Rodney Gallowglass of Gramarye, knighted by the king himself."

The king sat rigid. Then his voice hissed out. "A nobleman? A son of a lord, and his heir? And you strike against your own class?"

"Noblesse oblige," Gar replied, "and your dukes and earls have forgotten the obligations of their stations. We must remind them of those together, you and I."

"How dare you!" the king whispered. " 'You and I'? How dare you!" Suddenly, his voice turned calculating. "Of which obligations do you speak? Would you remind my dukes of their obligations to their king?"

"Yes, Majesty—to their king, but also to their serfs."

"Obligations to serfs! You would dare?"

"I would, and so would their councils. Who is your heir?"

The last question froze the king.

Gar waited.

Finally, His Majesty said, "A dutiful monarch must al-

ways open his ears to the plight of his people. I shall return
to the castle, Sir Gar. You may meet me in the audience
chamber in half an hour, with the people you speak of.''

Gar bowed his head. "As Your Majesty wishes.''

The soldiers opened a pathway back to the keep. The
king turned and rode back with as much dignity as he could
muster.

Inside the keep, he threw himself into a flurry of activity,
snapping out orders right and left. "Archers into the musi-
cian's loft! Spearmen dressed in butlers' livery! Knights—''

He stilled, realizing that there were no knights around
him—and, worse, that the few soldiers about him were listening very gravely, but doing absolutely nothing.

Then the sergeant gestured, and two soldiers stepped
forward, bowing. "Help His Majesty out of his armor,'' the
sergeant said. "Majesty, Sir Gar has sent us to see that you
are escorted to the throne with all the ceremony we can
muster.''

The king spat a string of curses that should have raised
blisters on the soldiers and singed the sergeant's beard.
They waited it out with grave, courteous expressions. In the
end, the king went with them.

As they were about to go into the throne room, a soldier
pushed his way through to Gar and Dirk. "Masters! Duke
Grenlach's loyal men overcame our rebels! He marches to
relieve the king, and all the soldiers who escaped our sweep
will rally to him!''

"Grenlach is a hundred miles away!'' Coll said, amazed.
"The word travels like lightning!''

"With every cell already standing? Word can travel faster
than any messenger, yes. Still, five hours is amazing.'' Gar
frowned. "A hundred miles, you say? And an army will do
well to march twenty miles a day—more likely only a dozen.
We have at least five days.'' He turned to Dirk. "Come, let
us present our arguments to His Majesty! We must be very
persuasive.''

"I thought you told me to leave the thumbscrews in the dungeon."

"Not *that* kind of persuasion!" Gar turned to the messenger. "How many men are dead?"

"Fewer than there would have been if this battle had begun, my master," the messenger said.

Gar stared at him for a moment. Then he said, "Yes." And, "That *is* the only thing that matters, isn't it?"

He turned back to face the throne room doors. "Let's try to make His Majesty see the sense in that."

16

"Your noblemen come to your gate, under a flag of truce," Gar informed the king.

The king narrowed his eyes. "You have not been up to the tower. How do you know this?"

"Because I have founded a secret society among your soldiers, and all the dukes' soldiers," Gar told him.

"Throughout your whole kingdom, in fact," Dirk put in. The king gave him a look that would have stretched him on the rack and made hot irons dance on his flesh, if he'd had any men who would have obeyed his command.

"Some you will know now," Gar said, "for they are the soldiers who are not bound and tied, but still bear arms. Still, you can't know who their leader is. That, too, is secret, and is known only to myself."

"Secret!" the king roared. "Nonsense! *You* are their leader, clearly and obviously! If I kill you, this rebellion ends!" He swung a huge blow with his sword.

A dozen men shouted and leaped to hold him, but Gar blocked with a quick movement of his own blade, then bound the king's sword and whipped it down. "Even if you could slay me, Majesty, another leader would take up the reins—and if you slew him, another would rise in his place. None but he would know of it, for all that the soldiers know is that orders are sent to them—they don't know who issues them."

"You are saying that it's impossible for me to kill the chiefs," the king interpreted.

Gar nodded. "And impossible, therefore, to kill the rebellion. There are simply too many people, and too few of them are known."

Surprisingly, the king didn't erupt again; he only nodded with a cold, calculating look. "Ingenious. I shall have to devote myself to discovering a way to foil the plan."

"You shall fail in that," Gar assured him. "For the moment, though, your companions in frustration approach your gate—and I think you may find you have more in common with your lords than you thought. Will you see them?"

"Whose idea is this parley?" the king demanded.

"Mine," Gar affirmed. "Their Graces are given little choice in the matter."

"Then I shall see them," the king declared.

Gar bowed. "Shall we open your gates and bring them into your keep?"

"Why ask me?" the king said bitterly. "Are you not the master here?"

"No," Gar told him firmly. "Neither I nor the soldiers' councils will try to tell you what you must do. We will only tell you what we will *not* do."

"And, therefore, what *I* cannot do," the king said dryly.

Gar bowed again. "But it is for you to say what you *will* do."

"Why, then, open the gates and let them in," the king said. "My lords and I may yet find some way to frustrate *your* designs."

Gar bowed and relayed the order.

The dukes rode in all together, with a sergeant beside them holding the white flag. They dismounted and went to the ornate chairs set out for them in the middle of the courtyard. Their own soldiers formed a crescent behind them, three rows deep. Before them, the king sat in a chair higher and more elaborate than any of theirs.

The dukes bowed, as protocol demanded. "Your Majesty!"

"My lords," the king returned, then gestured to Gar. "This ragtag free lance who dares to call himself the son of a lord is the author of all our misfortunes. I shall let him explain before I address you."

"I thank Your Majesty." Gar stepped forward at the foot of the throne, then turned to face the dukes. "My lords, your armies have made it clear to you that you cannot wage this war, for they refuse to fight it for you."

"Aye, you traitorous toad!" Trangray spat.

Gar ignored the insult. "However, if mere soldiers can prevent great dukes from fighting, surely all the lords together can prevent the king from doing anything they deem unjust."

The king stiffened, and the lords stared in surprise. Then they turned thoughtful, and the king narrowed his eyes as he glared at Gar.

Again, the giant ignored him. "You have but to refuse to obey his laws, and to tell him that you will not obey because they are unjust."

"Let me see if I understand you," Duke Trangray said. "You say that *we* can tell the king which laws to make and which to strike down?"

"You can."

"But he will send his armies against us," Duke Ekud said, with a shrewd gleam in his eye. "Do you say his armies cannot prevail against us, if we all act together?"

"He could never have that many knights and men," Gar confirmed.

"But what if the soldiers think his law *is* just?" Duke Ekud countered. "What if they refuse to fight?"

"Exactly," Gar said, with the tone of a teacher delighting in a pupil's insight. "From this day forth, you will never be able to rule without the consent of those you govern."

The lords broke into a furious chorus of denunciation. Gar waited it out, until finally the king broke it off with a clarion call. "My lords!"

The dukes fell silent, turning to him in surprise at such a tone of authority from one so young.

"It is clear that this outlander has hobbled us one and all," the king said, fuming. "How is this, Sir Gar? I am to ask my lords' permission for every little command I wish to issue?"

The dukes turned to Gar with a new, speculative gleam in their eyes.

"No, Your Majesty," Gar returned, "only for every law you would make, and every *major* action you would take. It is still for you to enforce the laws and conduct the affairs of your kingdom, as it always has been."

The king turned thoughtful. "So all is as it was, save that my lords can stop me from making laws or judgments they dislike?"

"And this without the risk of our knights or their soldiers?" Trangray asked.

Gar nodded. "In fact, it would be wise for you to set a definite month in which to meet on the plain outside the King's Town, so that the dukes and earls can discuss matters of common interest, and the king can consult with you on measures he needs to take for the welfare of the realm."

The king gave Gar a black glare, but the giant only said, "Such a meeting gives you an opportunity to explain your policies to your lords, Your Majesty, and to persuade them to support your course of action."

"Persuade!" the king exclaimed with indignation.

"Persuasion costs much less than fielding an army," Gar pointed out. "You might also reserve a month for consulting with the soldiers' councils and village councils from all over your kingdom—a meeting of councils, for talking. Call it a parliament."

The king's eye fired, and the dukes leaned forward in avid attention.

"Be aware that the spokesmen will not be the commanders," Gar told them. "They will be just that, spokesmen, people who speak for the councils, but not themselves in any position of authority. The real commanders of the councils will send minstrels to speak for them—messengers, if you will."

The dukes leaned back with looks of disappointment, and the fire in the king's eye died to be replaced by pure hatred, but Gar went on, unruffled. "The minstrels will not have the power to bargain—only to say 'no,' but not to say 'yes.'"

"Then what's the point in talking with them?" the king said in disgust.

"Because if you don't convince the lords, you may be able to convince the parliament—and they can forbid the lords' policies, or speak to their dukes in favor of your plans."

The dukes broke into an uproar, but the king's eye gleamed again. As the clamor subsided, he nodded. "So they will be able to forbid my laws, but their own peasant councils will be able to prevent theirs—or even to insist they accept my ideas."

"Not to insist," Gar said quickly, "no more than the lords can insist you adopt their course of action."

The lords exchanged a glance; they hadn't thought of that, but they were thinking of it now.

"The councils can petition their lords to do as Your Majesty suggests," Gar went on.

"Clever, Sir Gar, clever." The king leaned back in his great chair. "I begin to see some merit in your scheme after all."

"Then let the dukes draw up a charter, making clear

their rights and your obligations to them," Gar said, "and let all of you sign it, so that it becomes the law of the land."

The dukes all spoke in loud agreement. "Yes, indeed!" "An excellent idea!" "Only what is right, after all!"

The king scowled, not at all certain he liked having something in writing—but with so much feeling among the dukes, he had little choice. "Very well," he said grudgingly. "Let them bring me a draft of their charter tomorrow, that we can begin to haggle over its wording."

They had it there bright and early the next day, of course—Gar had handed them an example from another world, one called the Great Charter. They made a great number of changes, but they had the draft ready to spread out before the king when the sun rose. They argued about it for a week, first about the ideas, which really did little more than guarantee the dukes' liberties and rights, obligating them to fight for the king in return and to obey his laws—but their parliament had to approve those laws. Then they argued about the words, and finally about every comma and capital—but nine days after it began, the king and all his dukes and earls signed their own Great Charter. The soldiers went wild with joy, and so did the lords. The king grumbled, but his new sense of the importance of public support moved him to order his cooks to bring out whole carcasses of oxen and hogs and set them to roasting, while his butlers broached barrel after barrel of ale. The soldiers, the people of the town, and all the farm folk roundabout had a roaring party. But Gar, Dirk, and Coll made sure that one soldier in every ten stayed sober and vigilant, and that the king's men drank as much as the dukes' soldiers. The party ended without either side attacking the other, and the next day, when the dukes' soldiers had recovered from their hangovers, they packed up and began the journey home.

The dukes arrived back in their own demesnes in fine fettle, feeling that they had taught the upstart king his place—without spending a single soldier! They went up to the ramparts of their castle towers and surveyed each his own petty kingdom, reveling in a sense of power.

When they came down to their great halls, they found the spokesmen of the village councils waiting for them with charters of their own.

They signed them, of course—after furious rages and long bargaining sessions, after haranguing and bellowing and draft after draft after draft—but in the end, they signed their charters with the common people. They had no choice, for the spokesmen of the soldiers' councils stood right behind the villagers, and the soldiers behind their spokesmen.

When the charters were signed and the laws amended, the outlaws began to come out of the forests to accept the amnesty they offered.

Coll, though, didn't go back to his home village. He didn't even stay on Earl Insol's estates. He went back to the inn with Dirk and Gar right behind him, to find the players—and Ciare.

They arrived just as Enrico came limping up to the door on his crutch, and Dicea flew out of the inn to sail into him with a cry of joy. Enrico staggered back, trying to hold on to his crutch and hug Dicea both at the same time. Coll ran forward to catch him and steady him, then stood back, grinning—and looked up to see Ciare coming toward him, arms wide, with tears streaming down her face.

When they were done with frantic kissing and deep long kissing, she demanded, "Never leave me again! Never, never!"

"Never," Coll assured her, looking deeply into her eyes with a smile, "but do you really think I can become a player?"

Ciare stared at him as the meaning of his words sank in. "I had thought I would have to become a village wife to keep you," she whispered.

Coll shook his head. "A wild songbird might not die in a

cage, but half the beauty of its melody would be gone. I'll go where you go, sweeting."

Dirk nodded approvingly as they embraced again, their lips too busy for speech, and commented to Gar, "Might be good cover for the leader of a secret government, at that."

"An excellent cover," Gar agreed. "He can travel around the countryside without anyone wondering why—and who would suspect a vagabond of being a beggar king?"

"Always harder to find a moving target," Dirk agreed. "Now all we have to do is get him to agree."

That turned out to be the toughest part of the job altogether. "The lords will wipe out all the councils if somebody isn't working constantly to keep them going," Dirk argued. "Somebody has to take the ultimate responsibility for them, Coll—which means somebody has to be boss."

"If there's someone at the top of the pyramid of cells to give orders and keep them active," Gar explained, "the system will maintain itself. Now that the serfs have learned that they can unify and fight back, they won't forget."

"That doesn't mean it will all be clear sailing," Dirk warned. "The lords won't give up even this much of their power willingly. Some of them will try to avenge themselves on single serfs or even small groups of them. The councils will call for justice according to their charters, and will probably have to enforce it."

"Someone has to be issuing orders to make sure everyone learns how to use a quarterstaff and a bow, and keep them practicing."

Coll scowled, his massive reluctance weakening for the first time. "Yes, I can see that."

"The lords might even send out spies and bribe villagers to find out who the cell members are," Gar said, pressing his advantage. "Then they'll have their soldiers sweep down on them some night and murder them all."

"You're saying we must always have armies of outlaws in

the forests, ready to be called up to counter such a strike,"
Coll said grimly.

Dirk stared in surprise. "Yeah, great idea! I hadn't even
thought of it. You *do* have the talent you need for the job,
Coll."

"No, not I!" the serf cried in alarm.

"Who else?" Gar asked. "The lords will probably even
try attacking all the serfs together, to intimidate the councils and force them to identify themselves and surrender.
You'll have to be ready to call for them all to fight back. And
don't forget to save a large reserve in case it's a diversion."

"You see, there *has* to be somebody at the top to give
orders," Dirk insisted.

"But what if the lords should win!"

"Make sure they don't," Dirk said simply.

But Gar nodded with understanding. "It's a very real
danger, Coll. The history of old Earth, where the first people came from, tells of peasant rebellions every hundred
years or so, and tells also how the lords put them down with
brutal force. You're never done winning freedom. You have
to fight for it in every generation."

" 'The price of freedom is constant vigilance,' " Dirk
quoted, "so somebody always has to be a sentry, somebody
always has to be watching for signs of trouble and head it
off—or at least be ready for the fight when it comes."

"Worry," Gar counseled, "but don't worry *too* much.
None of those medieval peasant revolts were anywhere
nearly as well organized as yours. But the knights do have a
huge advantage."

Dirk nodded. "Horses, armor, and all the weapons—
plus constant practice. They're professionals, trained to war
from birth."

"So you have to make sure your peasants are trained
from birth, too," Gar reasoned.

"But how can we be sure the knights won't win?"

"You can't." Dirk's tone hardened. "You can never be sure—but your secret network gives you a very good chance of winning again and again, until a new generation of lords accepts the councils as part of the way the world is."

"But that network has to be efficiently and wisely run," Gar said, "which means there has to be somebody running it who understands how the system works, and how to use it."

"No peasant can know that!"

"*You* can," Dirk pointed out. "We've been explaining it to you step by step as we set it up. In fact, Coll, you're the only man in Aggrand who has even a chance of making it work."

"But I don't want it!" Coll protested. "All I want is to marry Ciare and spend my life with her and our children!"

Dirk turned to Gar. "That's the best kind of boss—the one who doesn't want the job, but loves the work."

"I don't!"

"Don't try to tell us that," Gar said with a hard smile. "You've thrown yourself into this whole task heart and soul, until you thought it was over."

"But it's never over," Dirk said softly, "not really. So if you want to be sure Ciare and your children are safe from the noblemen's whims, you'll have to keep the network going."

Coll stared, appalled as he realized Dirk spoke the truth.

"Has she said she'll marry you yet?" Dirk asked gently.

"I—haven't asked," Coll said through stiff lips. "Not really, not formally."

"Then you'd better ask her, hadn't you? And if she says 'yes,' tell her what she'll be getting into, and why you need to do it. *Then* if she still says she'll marry you, you'll know she's in love with you."

Coll asked her that afternoon—but he reversed the order.

17

◆

Ciare saw Coll coming back toward the stage and turned to him with a glad cry that froze on her lips when she saw the grim set of his face. She ran to him, hands out to press against his chest. "Coll! What troubles you?"

"Can you come aside with me?" Coll asked. "There's much I need to tell you."

"Of course." There were chores to do and her part in making dinner, but Ciare knew urgency when she saw it. Her friends would understand.

They paced out of the inn yard and into the center of the village common. Coll was silent until they were sitting on an old stump beneath a grandfather oak.

"They want me to be the master of all the serf councils," Coll said abruptly.

Ciare stared at him in shock, feeling that she was seeing his set profile for the first time. There was a strength there that she had never seen before, and the beginnings of wisdom. Her eyes filled with tears, for she suddenly understood what he had come to tell her, that a simple player-lass could never be a fit consort for the secret master of all the common folk. But she resolved on the instant not to hold him back—she knew that thwarted destiny makes a bitter man. Calling all her actress's skills to her aid, she forced a bright smile and said, "Oh, Coll, how wonderful!"

But he heard the tremor in her voice and turned to her, distressed. "If you don't want it, I'll tell them no! I still can—and a life with you is worth far more to me than any position!"

She stared at him, shocked again, then melted into his arms, pulling his head down for his lips to find hers, and let her mouth melt into his. When they finally broke apart, gasping, she managed to say, "But can't you be the Serf Master and still be my husband?"

"I can," he said gravely, looking straight into her eyes, "but it could be very dangerous. Spies might find me out and take us all to the torture. Worse, they might torture you to make me obey. I can't take that chance with your pain."

She reached out a trembling hand to touch his face and smiled through her tears. "Silly boy! Don't you see that I'd rather risk death than lose you? Besides, we've learned how to keep secrets, we player folk, and how to keep them from the knowledge of any town dweller or soldier anywhere! No, Coll, you can be the Serf Master *and* my husband—if you wish it."

"I don't wish to be Serf Master," he said truthfully, "but I *do* want to be your husband." He slipped down on one knee, taking both her hands between both of his, staring up at her with absolute concentration. "Ciare, will you marry me?"

She sat immobile for a moment, her eyes filling with tears, feeling that all her dreams had come true. Then she laughed and took his face in her hands to shower dozens of kisses all over his eyes, his cheeks, and finally his mouth. When they broke apart, she whispered, eyes still closed, "Yes, Coll. Oh, yes, I will marry you." Then she opened her eyes, staring at him almost indignantly. "But you must be Serf Master, too!"

His face was transfigured with joy, but he protested, "I have no property, no money—and I don't know how to be anything but a farmer and a soldier!"

"And a master of rebellion," she reminded him. "Well, then, since you know nothing else, you'll have to learn to be a player—if Master Androv will have you." She intended to make good and sure that he would.

Coll talked to Master Androv that very night (which didn't give Ciare much time to cozen the old fellow). "I know nothing of playacting," he said, "and I don't think I can learn. But I can help set up the stage and I can take tickets and quiet the rowdies in the audience—and I might come in handy if bandits attack you on the road."

"To be sure you would!" Androv said heartily, and clapped him on the shoulder. "You've been a stalwart member of this company already, Coll, and I'll be delighted to have you stay with us for good! Be sure, though, that even if you rarely go on stage, you'll earn your living in hard labor, just as you've said!"

Coll was amazed at such ready acceptance. "You're sure I won't be in the way?"

"In the way! Why, we'll wonder how we ever did without you!" Privately, Master Androv was also delighted to know that he wouldn't be losing Dicea, who was showing promise as a player and would have taken Enrico with her if she had left. But he was even more relieved to know that he'd be keeping Mama, who had turned out to have great skill, both with the needle and in keeping other people's spirits up.

So Coll announced their engagement over dinner that night, and the whole company cheered the couple and drank their health. Then Androv announced that Coll and his family would be traveling with them forever more, and they all cheered and drank again. One drink led to another, and before they knew it, they had a full-fledged party going.

Gar slipped away early, though. He went out into the fields and waited as a large parcel came floating down from the sky. The next day, he presented Coll with his wedding gift—a stack of playbooks printed out by his ship's computer, the best dramas, comedies, and tragedies that human playwrights had written since people learned to write. He and Dirk also presented Coll with enough gold coins to make both his eyes and his money belt bulge.

They stayed long enough to watch the wedding, three weeks later. Ciare insisted on being married in a church, which meant the company had to stay in one town long enough for the priest to read the banns three Sundays in a row. Gar knew they could never pull an audience that many weeks, especially since everyone in town had already seen every play in the company's repertoire while they were waiting for the war to end—so he paid the landlord for three weeks' room and board for everyone, and the whole company settled down for the first vacation they could ever remember.

It lasted until Coll gave Androv a copy of one of the plays Gar had given him—Shakespeare's *Measure for Measure*. He read it in one electrified sitting, then shouted all his players back onto the stage and made them begin rehearsals. By the time the Church was satisfied that no one in town knew any reason why Coll and Ciare couldn't marry, the play was ready to perform.

Even then, the priest would only marry them in the portico in front of the church, because they were players. But the other players costumed the bride in splendor and decorated bride and groom both with flowers, not to mention the pillars and, nearly, the priest. Finally falling into the spirit of the occasion, he smiled and prompted them.

"Do you, Coll, take this woman, Ciare, to be your lawfully wedded wife, to have and to hold, for better or for worse, in sickness or in health, till death do you part?"

" 'I do,' " Dirk muttered behind him.

"I do!" Coll gasped.

"And do you, Ciare, take this man Coll to be your lawfully wedded husband, to have and to hold, for better or for worse, in sickness and in health, until death do you part?"

"I do!" Ciare declared, her face radiant.

"Then I now pronounce you man and wife." The priest lowered his voice. "You may kiss the bride."

Coll did, and Dicea cast a shy but speculative look at Enrico, who beamed back at her while the rest of the company erupted in cheers and led the bride and groom away from the church to a festival in the innyard where they had set up their stage. Everyone drank deeply and danced wildly, then with gay hilarity and many ribald comments ushered the newlyweds to the best bedroom the inn had to offer.

They emerged as the morning shadows stretched long across the grass of the village green, and Coll sobered at once, seeing the looks on the faces of Dirk and Gar. He hurried over to them, Ciare on his arm. "What troubles you, my friends?"

"Only that we have to leave," Gar told him. "We've waited to say good-bye to you, but the time has come."

A sudden void seemed to open inside Coll, and panic filled it. "But how shall we manage without you? What if the lords rise against us?"

"You know what to do." Gar laid a hand on his shoulder. "We've taught you all you need to know. Just remember to be cautious always, and suspect every deed any lord does."

Dirk nodded. "You can manage it. Have a good life, you two." For a moment, his gaze rested on Ciare, and his face seemed gaunt with longing. Then he shook himself and turned back to clap Coll on the shoulder. "You lucky peasant!" he said in a husky voice. "You lucky, wealthy man!" Then he turned and strode away toward the forest.

They watched him go, and Ciare asked, mystified, "Why did he call you wealthy?"

"Because I have you." Coll clasped her firmly against his side and lowered his cheek to rest against her hair. A great peace, an amazing sense of contentment, rose to fill the void where there had been only panic minutes before.

"You are wealthy indeed, in all the ways that I wish I were." Gar lifted Ciare's hand to kiss it, then looked straight into her eyes. "May you have healthy children and a long life, my friends—and may the memory of these days of love sustain you whenever hard times come, all through your life."

"They will," Ciare whispered, her eyes filled with tears. "Farewell, O my friend!"

"Farewell," Coll whispered.

"Fare well through all your days." Then Gar bowed and turned away, striding fast to catch up with Dirk.

"I hope they find their loves," Ciare said, nestling closer against Coll.

"So do I," he breathed, "but I thank Heaven all the more that I have found mine!" He turned to kiss her, long, lingering, and lasting.

When darkness fell, Dirk and Gar stepped out of the trees into a wide forest meadow to watch a small black circle form overhead, one that grew steadily larger and larger still, until it blotted out all the stars. Then, abruptly, it was no longer a circle in the sky, but a huge circular spaceship that lowered itself into the meadow, nearly filling it, with only twenty feet or so between ship and trees. A boarding ramp lowered, leading up to light, and a voice said, "Ready to board, gentlemen."

"Thank you, Herkimer." Gar led the way up the ramp.

They came into the lighted lock. The ramp closed behind them, and the voice said, "Welcome home, Magnus. Welcome home, Dirk."

"Home it is!" Dirk threw himself down into a lounger. "Ah, the blessings of the modern world! You can have the shower first, Gar. I think I'll just sit here a while, and soak up some sybaritic luxury."

He knew very well that there were four showers aboard. Gar took a drink from the dispenser and handed it to Dirk. "You might want to try this with it." He headed toward a shower cubicle, calling, "Lift off, Herkimer." He felt no change in weight as he shucked his clothes and stepped into the shower, but he knew that the spaceship was rising again into the night, up and up into orbit.

He came out of the shower to find Dirk's glass and lounger empty. Magnus pulled on modern clothing, took a drink of his own, sat down in the lounger, and watched the planet Maltroit grow smaller and smaller in the viewscreen.

Dirk came out, wearing shirt and breeches of soft, shimmering, synthetic cloth. He tapped another glassful and took the lounger next to Gar's, watching the planet turn from a huge presence above them into a swirling disk in front of them. "Strange to think it's over."

"Over for us," Gar returned. "Just begun, for Coll and Ciare."

"Think we might come back to see them again someday?"

"Not really," Gar said regretfully. "It's a big galaxy, after all—a very big galaxy. But I think the Wizard might look in on him from time to time."

"He might, at that." Dirk took a sip, then said, "Do you think he'll ever figure out that the Wizard was you?"

"Only if he suspects I'm a mind reader," Gar replied, "and since he's probably never even heard the word 'telepath,' I doubt he'll ever suspect anything."

"And since he doesn't know what a telekinetic is, he'll never figure out that there was anything to that prison window coming loose other than old mortar . . ."

"It wasn't," Gar told him. "It was only ten years old, and hard as the holes in Hell!"

". . . or why a handful of men were able to start the player's cart moving, or why it rolled so easily, or how you knew where an enemy was going to swing next, or . . ."

"Spare me the catalog," Gar groaned. "Remember, you yourself said I would be silly not to use the advantage I had."

"And I'll say it again, anytime you start developing scruples." Dirk fell silent again, sipping his drink, watching the screen, and feeling the tension roll off him. Maltroit grew smaller and smaller until it occupied only about a third of the screen's area. There, it stabilized.

"We have achieved orbit," Herkimer told them.

"So." Dirk rolled his glass between his palms, then looked up at Gar. "Whose world shall we save next?"

TOR
BOOKS The Best in Fantasy

ELVENBANE • Andre Norton and Mercedes Lackey
"A richly detailed, complex fantasy collaboration."—Marion Zimmer Bradley

SUMMER KING, WINTER FOOL • Lisa Goldstein
"Possesses all of Goldstein's virtues to the highest degree."—*Chicago Sun-Times*

JACK OF KINROWAN • Charles de Lint
Jack the Giant Killer and *Drink Down the Moon* reprinted in one volume.

THE MAGIC ENGINEER • L.E. Modesitt, Jr.
The tale of Dorrin the blacksmith in the enormously popular continuing saga of Recluce.

SISTER LIGHT, SISTER DARK • Jane Yolen
"The Hans Christian Andersen of America."—*Newsweek*

THE GIRL WHO HEARD DRAGONS • Anne McCaffrey
"A treat for McCaffrey fans."—*Locus*

GEIS OF THE GARGOYLE • Piers Anthony
Join Gary Gar, a guileless young gargoyle disguised as a human, on a perilous pilgrimage in pursuit of a philter to rescue the magical land of Xanth from an ancient evil.